BACKFIRED

J T FISHER

Author's Tranquility Press
MARIETTA, GEORGIA

Copyright © 2022 by J T Fisher

All rights reserved. No part of this publication may be reproduced, distributed or transmitted in any form or by any means, including photocopying, recording, or other electronic or mechanical methods, without the prior written permission of the publisher, except in the case of brief quotations embodied in critical reviews and certain other noncommercial uses permitted by copyright law. For permission requests, write to the publisher, addressed "Attention: Permissions Coordinator," at the address below.

J T Fisher/Author's Tranquility Press
2706 Station Club Drive SW
Marietta, GA 30060
www.authorstranquilitypress.com

Ordering Information:
Quantity sales. Special discounts are available on quantity purchases by corporations, associations, and others. For details, contact the "Special Sales Department" at the address above.

Backfired/J T Fisher
Paperback: 978-1-959197-93-5
eBook: 978-1-959197-94-2

Tis better to have loved and lost than never to have loved at all.

~~Alfred Lord Tennyson

This book is dedicated to Rob Berger who encouraged me to stretch beyond my own boundaries to find new horizons.

And to all who have ever suffered unrequited love. May you have the patience to abide... someone is out there waiting for you.

Contents

Chapter 1 1

Chapter 2 10

Chapter 3 22

Chapter 4 39

Chapter 5 48

Chapter 6 57

Chapter 7 70

Chapter 8 87

Chapter 9 99

Chapter 10 120

Chapter 11 125

Chapter 12 140

Chapter 13 150

Chapter 14 166

Chapter 15 170

Chapter 16 180

Chapter 17 190

Chapter 18	194
Chapter 19	212
Chapter 20	228
Chapter 21	239
Chapter 22	256
Chapter 23	267
Chapter 24	273
Chapter 25	289
Chapter 26	300
Chapter 27	311
Chapter 28	319
ABOUT THE AUTHOR	323

Chapter 1

"Ma'am settle down. Everything is going to be okay. Shhh." Officer Logan put his arm around the petite woman to calm her shivering and sobbing. His squad car sat on the street, blue lights still flashing as the ambulance pulled away. Two other squad cars had arrived in the last few minutes and a CSI van was parked across the street, half on the curb, and half in the driveway of the neighbor. "Now, you were saying?" The officer stood there looking at Jeanie Wright, waiting for an answer. She had none. For a few seconds, she didn't even remember why she had called them.

Or was it even she who had called them? She pushed her slight weight off the hood of the car to try to stand up without leaning, but her legs were still wobbly.

"Oh, yeah, right. Where was I? Do we know who did this?" Jeanie's brain was firing thoughts off in all directions. She couldn't remember what she was telling the cop before she fell apart. There was so much going on at once. "Is it possible to go inside and get a cold drink and sit down. I'm feeling a little light headed. Jeanie looked at him hopefully, trying to regain her composure.

"I imagine it would be okay. You might want to change your blouse while you're in there." The officer representing the Broward County Sheriff's office was trying to be as polite as possible. He towered over Jeanie's demure frame, overpowering her in stature, and he knew she was shaking from whatever had just happened in her driveway, but he still had to take her to the precinct for questioning. "Go in and change and get a cold drink. But then we have to go to the station to fill out some paperwork about what happened here tonight."

"What time is it now? I hardly remember what happened." Jeanie started to weep but wasn't sure where the tears were coming from. "Last I remember was getting that call from the Keys and then waiting out on the front porch to be picked up by my friend

Nick. We were going to go out for coffee while I waited for them to call me back." She looked down at her blouse, reacting as if it was the first time she noticed the blood.

She started screaming again. "Oh my God, what happened? Is that my blood?" Jeanie grabbed at her chest and then her neck. Then she reached for her face, gently patting all around it and looking at her hands frantically, looking for new blood.

"You're fine, ma'am. Just in shock. We had the paramedics give you a check before they left. They said you might want to get something to help you sleep tonight, but otherwise, you're fine. Is there someone we can call?" The officer tried to speak calmly and soothingly.

"Oh, okay. No, nobody. I don't remember." Jeanie turned toward the house. "Nothing happened inside, right? I mean, nobody went in the house. I have my keys right here." She reached into her purse and her keys were right where she usually keeps them. Jeanie continued up the path back to the porch. It was dimly lit as it was fully night time now. She thought to herself how she had been bugging Carl to get brighter bulbs for months and he never listens to her.

Jeanie slipped the key into the shiny lock in the oversized front door and turned it slowly. Something was terribly wrong, but she still felt so removed from the events of the evening that she didn't know what it was. She slowly opened the door and the whine of the hinge again reminded her of the constant nagging to Carl to oil the hinges. It was always like that. She had to ask and ask until she got good and angry. And then it became a thing. And things always became fights.

Jeanie climbed the long staircase up to the bedroom, all the while thinking to herself that the house was too big for the two of them. The kids had been gone for almost ten years already, having left for college vowing never to return except for visits. What did they need four bedrooms for anyway? Jeanie reached the master suite and went past the dresser into the walk-in closet. She reached up and pulled down her college sweatshirt. When she spun around and got her first look in a mirror, a full length one at that, she was horrified. Her pink tunic was splashed with blood over the right shoulder and across the right side of the front of her tunic and jeans. There was also some dried blood on the side of her neck and on her face. She leaned in close to the mirror and noticed that it was even in her hair.

"I don't care what they say. They may be in a hurry, but I'm taking a shower. This can't be Carl's blood, or is it? Oh my god, what happened tonight?"

Jeanie turned on the shower and stripped down, tossing her clothes, all of them, into the hamper. Pausing for a moment, she slowly lifted her right hand to her face, sniffing hesitantly, hoping that she wouldn't smell anything like gunpowder, not that she knew what it smelled like.

Jeanie was cognizant enough to know that Erma, her housekeeper, would be at work tomorrow, and she would be able to take care of all the stains. She stepped into the shower and quickly soaped up, rinsed and then shampooed. She allowed the hot water to run down her back for a few extra minutes, as the chronology of the night started to come back to her. She still didn't know how or why it happened, but by the time she got out of the shower, she was ready to tell the police what little she knew about what happened in her driveway just a few hours earlier, and everything she knew that led up to it.

Dried and clothed, Jeanie tripped her way back down the stairs. When she reached the bottom, she twirled around down the hall in the opposite direction of the front door, toward the kitchen. The motion sensor lights went on as she passed the archway. She thought back to the day Carl installed this cute little feature. He had put in a floor lit pathway directly to the refrigerator so that he wouldn't have to turn on any lights when he got up for a middle of the night snack. She laughed out loud. "Damn if the thing doesn't still work!"

Jeanie opened the refrigerator and grabbed a plastic container full of homemade cookies as well as a six-pack of flavored water. She figured a little honey would go a long way. Maybe it would go faster with some refreshments, *unless they think I did something wrong.*

With her care package in tow, Jeanie retraced her steps down the hallway toward the front door but did not make it before the tall officer was already looking for her, first banging on the wood door, followed by ringing the bell. "Ma'am, it really is time that we be going."

"I'm sorry, I had to shower. I felt so dirty," offered Jeanie.

"We'll need to take the blouse with us., if you don't mind retrieving it." The officer pulled a plastic bag out of the back pocket of his uniform trousers. "Please, ma'am. Put the blouse in this so we can type and reference it."

"Not a problem." Jeanie started back up the stairs. "But I don't know why you would want such a thing. There was blood all over everything."

"Yes ma'am. Just need to be sure of how many different blood types there were at the scene, that's all."

A half minute later, Jeanie returned carrying both the blouse and her jeans. She extended her hand to the officer, offering the bag to him and awkwardly asked him how she would get home from the police station if she went there with him.

"Not to worry ma'am. We'll have an officer bring you home after we finish whatever questioning and paperwork we need to complete." The officer paused, realizing that the woman with whom he was speaking was scared and shocked. "We will be sure you will be well taken care of and see to all of your needs. And we can even have an officer stay with you awhile if necessary.

Jeanie hardly heard the officer. Mesmerized by the flashing lights she was glancing around, noticing all her neighbors poking their heads out from behind their front doors or living room drapes, trying to see what was happening. "Huh? What? I'm sorry, I wasn't paying attention."

"We need to get going if we're going to get you back home at a reasonable hour." The officer took Jeanie by the elbow and led her to the only squad car parked on the street and not blocked in. He opened the front passenger side of the car and ushered her in. After he closed the door, Jeanie let out a sigh of relief that she wasn't thrown into the back seat with all her neighbors watching.

"Thank you for being so kind to me. I'm really at a loss as to what happened. And I do appreciate you letting me sit up front instead of in the back like a common criminal. I don't THINK I did anything wrong, but I really don't know exactly what happened. The last thing I remember is going outside to wait for Nick to pick me up. We were going to go out for a cup of coffee. Next thing I know, you are all here."

"Well," began the officer, "we're going to try to piece everything together to find that out." He started up the car and slowly backed up, and then pulled out into the middle of the street. Jeanie looked over her shoulder out the window, watching as the officers they left behind began cordoning off the driveway to her home including the walkway to her front door. In bold letters she was able to make out the words 'crime scene.' She watched as the scene grew smaller and smaller in the mirror, and then slumped back down in her seat for the ride to the local police station, the ride took a mere fifteen minutes, but to Jeanie it seemed like an eternity. She rested her head against the window glass and concentrated on the sound of her own heartbeat which, surprisingly to her, was coming from her neck, rather than her heart.

Chapter 2

Officer Logan led Jeanie in through the back door of the Police station building after he had helped her climb out of the front seat. She had become disoriented as if she had forgotten why she was with him. She was frozen with fear. The police officer had to lift her out of the car and put his arm around waist to help her walk. She had faltered on the steps, so he decided to avoid a fall, and lead her up the handicap ramp instead.

"It's a short walk to where we can sit down and get a cup of coffee or tea." The officer tried to sound reassuring, but this woman was making it difficult. He found himself pushing her from behind. Jeanie was slow to move, paralyzed with anxiety.

"Can I make a phone call before we go in there?"

"Ma'am, you are not being interrogated here. You are not a prisoner, if that's what you are thinking." Officer Logan realized then that maybe her fear was because she thought she was being arrested. "Feel free to make a call. We will need to examine your phone at some point before you go home."

Jeanie stopped cold. She grabbed at her chest and patted down her breasts. Her movements then became frantic. She reached behind her and smacked her back pockets and then her front. She swung her hoodie pockets around and dug into both sides with each hand. "I can't find my phone. I can't find it."

"Did you check your purse?"

"I never put it in there," Jeanie declared.

"Do yourself a favor and look before you panic," said Officer Logan, calmly.

Jeanie allowed her purse strap to slip off her shoulder down to her left hand and reached in with her right. She rummaged around for only a few seconds before she sheepishly slid out her phone. "I'm embarrassed. I must not have been thinking when I put myself together to come here. I almost NEVER put my phone in my purse. Ever since I had my purse snatched a few years ago, about the only thing I keep in there is make-up."

"No worries, ma'am. You go ahead and make your call, and I'll go and get us some coffee. How do you like yours?"

"Just like it is. Black. No cream, no sugar, thank you." Jeanie turned her back toward the wall and dialed Carl's number and nervously put the phone to her ear. Before she could clear her short brown hair away to hear clearly, the sound of his voice mail message had already started. "Shoot!" Her heart sank. She listened quietly to the sound of his voice. This was the eighth time she had done that since she had gotten the call from the Marine Patrol in the Keys.

"Are you ready?" Officer Logan had already returned with two cups of coffee and another man. "This is Detective Harris. He's going to sit with us and has a few questions to ask you, so we can figure out what happened tonight."

"Oh, okay." Jeanie followed the two men down to a small room a bit further down the hall. She again stopped, rigid in her small frame. A small sign hung on the wall just to the left of the door frame at eye level. Jeanie eyes fixed on the grey plastic sign with the small white letters. She stared at the word 'interrogation' for what seemed like a full minute. The pulsating in her neck had started again, just as it had in the squad car.

"Ma'am, can we..." Officer Logan had been holding the door open. Detective Harris was already in the room, sitting at a brushed stainless-steel table.

Jeanie came back to the present. "I thought I wasn't going to be arrested. Didn't you say I wasn't arrested? Why am I being interrogated?" She was hesitant to go through the door.

"Oh, the sign." The officer rolled his eyes. "I'm sorry. It's just a room where we can sit down and talk quietly. Believe me, you don't want to go into the squad room. It's way too noisy in there." He motioned for her to come in. "C'mon. It'll be okay."

Jeanie slowly walked through the archway of the interrogation room. The first thing she noticed was the table. It reminded Jeanie of a professional gourmet kitchen or an operating room, neither of which made her feel very comfortable. Antiseptic, cold and unfeeling. She slowly wandered over to a steel chair on the opposite side of the table and slid it out. Her body slithered down into the seat as she softly dropped her purse strap on the back of the chair. She reached across the table and pulled a cup of coffee toward her. "Wait!" She sat up in her chair. "I left some cookies and water in the car."

"I'll run out and get it. You sit still." Officer Logan jumped up and left the room.

Detective Harris leaned forward, rolling up the sleeves of his light blue oxford shirt. He didn't actually roll them up, Jeanie thought. He shoved them up, like Carl does. He then put his elbows on the cold steel table and began to talk.

"So, Mrs. Wright, is it?" Detective Harris asked as he looked down at the paperwork in front of him. "What is it that you remember about what happened this evening?" He looked up ever so slightly, yet making eye contact with her over his glasses, which sat precariously on the tip of his nose.

Jeanie was sipping her coffee when he spoke. She put the cup down and nervously answered the best she could. "Not very much, I'm afraid." She drew a labored and long breath and sat back in her chair. "Is Nick dead? Nick is dead. Isn't he?"

The detective rolled his eyes knowing that this discussion was going to be difficult. His record would stand, and he would likely miss dinner again. "Yes, he's dead. I kind of need you to start a little earlier than that." He dropped the paper on the table and then used the middle finger of his left hand to push his glasses up on his face. "First, what is your relationship to the victim and why was he at your house?"

Jeanie let out a big sigh. "Well, I've known Nick since high school. Or, I should say I knew him as far back as high school."

"Wait, what?" Detective Harris seemed confused. "Those are two uniquely different statements. Had you maintained a relationship with him all along? Or has it been more like he's been in and out of your purview off and on since high school."

"Okay, let me try to clear that up." Jeanie sat forward again, fiddling with her coffee cup. "Nick and I went to the same high school. We sort of knew each other then. I think he wanted to know me better, but I wasn't too interested, ya know what I mean?" She paused. "He, I guess you could say, had a crush on me. Used to ride his bike back and forth in front of my house trying to get a glimpse. I would watch him from our living room, from behind the curtains, and wait till he was gone before I would leave."

"Did he ever catch you coming or going? I mean, is that why you avoided him? Did he give you a reason to avoid him?"

"Not really. I just didn't want to date him. I had a crush on someone else." Jeanie thought back and was remembering her high school days. She remembered Nick back then. He was kind of a weirdo. "Nick was into some strange things like science fiction and alien sightings. He had really bad acne, too. He played the tuba in the marching band." She stopped talking for a second, realizing that she might be saying things that might offend the detective. "He just didn't do it for me. My crush, then later my boyfriend, was on the baseball team, the debate team and liked to go dancing. I loved going out dancing."

"So, did you end up marrying your high school sweet heart?" The detective wanted to get past this stuff as fast as possible and get down to the details of the crime scene.

"No, not him. My husband, though, does like dancing, or he used to anyway." Suddenly Jeanie realized she had forgotten about her situation with Carl. "Excuse me, detective, but may I make a quick phone call? I mean, I need to dial his number to see if he picks up."

"Go ahead. Do you want me to leave the room?"

"Only if he picks up." Julie put her phone on the table and pushed the redial button and the speaker button, and then waited. In three seconds, the familiar sound of Carl's voice was echoing in the sparsely furnished room. "Hey, it's Carl. Can't pick up. Please leave a message."

Jeanie smacked her thumb on the little red receiver button. Frustrated, she picked up the phone and handed it to the detective. "Officer Logan said you all needed to examine this?"

At the exact moment she finished her question, Logan pushed open the door of the interrogation room carrying the cookies and the six-pack of water. "I'm back. Yes, we need to get a list of the numbers you called and who called you. If you sign a release, we can just download it. It will help in our investigation."

The detective took the phone from Jeanie and put it in his pocket in one sweeping motion. He glanced at her over his glasses once again, as if he was trying to remember where he had met her before, a quizzical expression on his face. She looked directly at him. Jeanie wasn't one to back down. "What are you looking at?"

"Nothing in particular." He pushed his glasses back up on his face once again. "Now, tell me again, how you know the victim?" He was prepared to take notes this time, and fully expected to hear the same exact story.

"As I said," Jeanie began, "I knew Nick in high school, although not intimately. He had a crush on me, but I wasn't interested in dating him. He asked me out a couple of times, but I said no."

"And you never went out with him?"

"No." Jeanie was getting frustrated. "I already told you that I had a crush on someone else and started dating him." Jeanie talking for a moment, a glazed look washed over her face. "Unless you want to count one silly dance, I invited him to, kind of out of pity."

"So, then, why are you still in contact with him now so much so that he was parked in your driveway?"

"Oh, right." Jeanie seemed to snap back to the present. "That was his Cutlass. Man, that was the same car he had in high school. It must be what, forty years old?" She tilted her head back as if to figure out the math.

"Ma'am?" Now the detective was frustrated. "Can you answer the question?"

"Oh right, I'm sorry." Again, Jeanie reoccupied the present. "I was remembering when Nick first got that car. He kind of used it to try to bribe me into going out with him." She sat up in her chair and took a quick sip of her coffee. "I reconnected with Nick about six months ago. I've been working on the planning committee for our 40th high school reunion, and he called with a question. He's been kind of hanging around a lot since. I've had coffee or lunch with him two or three times since then, but that's really it."

"And why was he at your house tonight?"

"I'm not really sure." Jeanie stopped talking and stared at the detective's pocket, at the top corner of her phone which was peeking out of the pocket.

Again, she felt the thumping in her throat. "I had gotten a call from Key West. My husband is on a fishing excursion down there and they got a call from his boat." Her breathing became fast and shallow. "They said they got the call but then lost the signal. They would call me when they knew more. I got scared and I think I called Nick. I don't know why."

"Ma'am, can I ask you a personal question? Is it possible that you are having some sort of relationship with the victim?"

"Absolutely not!" Jeanie was indignant. "I'm a married woman. And faithful. His was just the first number that came up on my recent call list. You see, we are new to the area, and none of my girlfriends are around this time of night on a Saturday night. I didn't want to upset my kids in case its nothing. That's a terrible thing to insinuate." Jeanie's face was scarlet with anger, or was it embarrassment? Her words were choppy, some indistinguishable.

"I apologize; however, this is a formal investigation and sometimes I have to ask uncomfortable questions." His glasses had slid down his nose again, so the detective sat back in his chair, took his glasses off and carefully laid them on the table next to his notebook. "This is not to suggest that there was some sort of love triangle or that you did anything wrong. I just need to get the facts."

"Well, I think it's rather rude of you to even ask." She slumped back into the chair, feeling the heat of tears welling up. In an attempt to quash this, she tried to change the subject. "Is my phone vibrating in your pocket?"

Placing his hand across his chest, the detective simply said, "No," He waited for her to gather herself before he continued. Crossing his arms across his chest, the detective began a slow and steady rocking in his chair. The heels of the front legs of his chair lifted ever so slightly off the waxen floor, and when they touched town, the clicking they made were in lock-step with the ticking of the simple wall clock that hung over his shoulder on the dank grey wall.

Jeanie took a deep breath. "Well... Let me start from the beginning by telling you what I knew of him back in high school. It was a long time ago, but..."

CHAPTER 3
(Forty years prior...)

"Nick, where are you going this time?" Nick Lefton's mother Sheila was irritated at the undue attention her son was giving this girl. Every afternoon after school he was riding his bicycle up and down the street in front of her house, but he never was able to get up the nerve to ask her out on a date. It was almost as if he was stalking her. She dried her hands on a dish towel and called after him again. "Nick, did you hear me?"

"Yes, mom. I heard you." Nick rolled his eyes as he took one last glance in the hall mirror and brushed his long bangs to the side. He knew Jeanie would never even look at him with his acne covered face, but he still thrilled at the sight of her. He was going back to her street once again, even if only for a glance of her, coming or going, getting in or out of the car, sitting on the front porch swing with a girlfriend or even another boyfriend. He didn't care. "I'll be home in time for dinner," he shouted back over his shoulder.

Nick kicked open the front door of his Pickwick Estates home, thrusting the screen door open with his shoulder and letting them both slam behind him. His bike sat leaning against and chained to the rusted slider swing that was uncared for in twenty years. That swing always embarrassed him. He never wanted to bring friends home through the front door of his house. He unlocked the bike, tossing the chain and lock on the seat of the swing. The sound of metal hitting metal echoed under the length of the entire porch and rang in Nick's ears for several seconds after he had hopped up on the seat and was peddling down the walkway of his house and out into the street.

Please be home, please be home, he thought to himself. Nick's tall and thin physique made him appear awkward trying to peddle down the street. His legs were too long to be graceful in motion and his upper torso had to curl over, elbows bent, to fit over the handlebars. *I need a new bike, he thought. This one is too small.* His mind wandered to Jeanie.

She was a goddess, in his opinion. She was medium height for most girls, but that made her short next to him. It made him feel as though he towered over her, her protector. She had the most beautiful long blond hair. It was thick and flowing, and always beautifully kept. He often dreamt about running his fingers through it, imagining that it would feel like silk. And her complexion was smooth and velvety. Sometimes, during geometry class, when the noon day sun came through the window, he would peek over her and the tiny little hairs on her cheeks would remind him of peach fuzz. Nick would laugh at himself every time his mother put a peach in his lunch box, because he would always softly rub it up against the side of his face, envisioning it was Jeanie's face.

Lost in his thoughts, Nick didn't see the station wagon that ran through the red light, and he didn't have time to avoid an accident. Thankfully, the car swerved and clipped his rear tire only slightly. The impact was enough to throw Nick from his bike, landing him softly in a hedge along the sidewalk. The car sped on, leaving Nick behind, bruised and scratched up, with a mangled bike. He scrambled out of the brush and looked around. There was nobody offering to stop and help. His bike disfigured; he too was now unpresentable.

"Shit!" Nick picked up his bicycle and tried to wheel it along the sidewalk to see if it was rideable.

The rear tire was bent enough that it wouldn't pass through the frame without getting stuck. He resigned himself to the fact that he would not be seeing Jeanie that day, nor would he have a quick way to get to school until he could either get the tire fixed or get a new bike. Trying to see the bright side, which went against his nature, he saw this as an opportunity to get a bigger bicycle at least. After considerable maneuvering, he figured out a way to lift the rear end of the bike with one arm and steer it with the other as he made his way home.

"Mom, I'm going to need to get a new bike." He yelled to his mother as he let the front door slam behind him. He offered no other explanation and then skipped up the stairs, two at a time, to his room, on the second floor of the split-level home. Before she could respond, Nick had slammed his bedroom door shut.

Once safely in his room, Nick pulled out a folder from under his mattress. He flipped open the cover. In the left side pocket, he kept an envelope of cash he had amassed from various jobs he had held: lawn cutting, baby-sitting and a few other odd jobs around the neighborhood. His parents gave him a small allowance, and he never spent any money because he never went out on dates. In the right pocket he had saved a half dozen photographs of Jeanie. Some were from school, and a few were Polaroid pictures he had taken of her from afar, ones she didn't know about.

Nick opened the cash envelope to see if he had enough money to buy a much better bicycle, in case he got a hard time from his dad about buying a new one. Getting money from his father for anything, including the dentist or the doctor, was almost impossible. "I work very hard for that money and you go around spending it willy-nilly. What to you need to go to the doctor for?" Nick laughed to himself, thinking about the possible answers he would give to his scrooge father. "Uh, dad, I broke my leg and I'm bleeding to death?"

There was approximately two hundred dollars in the envelope. Nick figured that would buy him a decent ten-speed bike, but maybe not the top brand. At least he wouldn't be embarrassed riding it to school. He folded up the money and put it back in the envelope, and then slipped it back in the left pocket of the folder. He then took out the pictures of Jeanie.

Nick tossed the folder on the floor beside his bed and stretched out with the stack of pictures in his hand. He took his time looking at each picture, imagining himself next to her in each one. His right hand slowly moved down toward his belt. He slipped his hand down his pants and began fondling himself, his eyes closed. 'Mmmmmmmm, oh Jeanie..."

A knock at his door interrupted Nick before he had a chance to finish what he was doing. He quickly rolled on his side and drew his knees up to mask his erection, while at the same time, slipping the photographs under his pillow. In a cracked and surprisingly high voice, he tried to sound natural, "Come in."

"I didn't hear you come in, but Dad said your bike is all bent up on the porch. Are you okay?' Nick's mom was a typical 1970's mother, attempting to be hip but still caught somewhat in the sixties. She wasn't quite a hippie, but not anyone's grandmother, either.

"I'm fine, mom." Nick was visibly aggravated. "I got clipped by some guy who ran a red light. I hit the bushes. I'm not hurt. Just my bike." His erection was still pressing against his jeans, so he couldn't stretch his legs out, much less stand up.

"Are you sure? Let me take a look at you."

"No, mom!" Nick was indignant. "And I don't appreciate you just barging in my room like this either. You didn't even knock. What if I did that to you?"

Nick's mom sighed. His outburst communicated to her, in no uncertain terms, that her son was fine. "Okay, so you're fine. Sorry I bothered you." She turned around to leave but took the opportunity to exert her parental authority by adding, "and don't talk to me in that tone of voice." And then she was gone.

Nick waited for a few seconds to be sure she was gone. His mother had a habit of including addendums to her reprimands. Her afterthoughts were always stronger than the first things that come to her mind. He listened carefully for returning footsteps, but he heard none. Slowly he stretched out his legs. He had been caught jerking off by his dad once, but his dad thought it was funny. He didn't want to find out how his mother would react.

Nick slid the pictures of Jeanie out from under his pillow and decided to put them away for now. He kept the one of her on her porch swing, reading, held tightly in his hand. Falling back on the pillow, he stared at it for a few seconds. Eventually, he sat up and put it on the back of his night table, facing his bed so it would seem like she was there in the room, with him. After a few more seconds of living in his dream world, he got up, brushed his hair and tripped down the stairs to find out how long it would be until dinner.

When he reached the kitchen, his mom was just pulling down plates to set the table. That was a good sign. He offered to help, which was his way of apologizing to his mother for sassing her. It always worked. He took the plates from her and grabbed the pile of silverware that she had already counted out and carried it all into the dining room. He was startled to find his father already sitting at the dining room table.

"Hello Dad."

"Hello, son." Norman Lefton looked up from his paper. "I understand you were hit by a car on your bike today. Did you at least do more damage to the other guy?"

"I don't know dad, he drove away." Nick hated how his father always expected him to be this warrior type. "I was thrown into the bushes, so I didn't really even see the kind of car it was. I just know it was light-colored." Nick put the dishes and silverware down at the opposite end of the table from where his father was seated. "I gotta go get napkins."

Before his father had a chance to ask another question, Nick had turned on his heels and returned to the kitchen. "Mom, could you tell Dad to lay off me?" He reached over her while she was pouring vegetables into a bowl, to get into the cabinet that held the paper goods. "He's making it into a whole big thing. And can you see if he'll give me a few bucks towards a new bike?"

Sheila sighed. "I'll try."

Nick took four dinner napkins from the napkin holder and tried to fold them into swans. He resented the fact that they had to have dinner in the dining room every damn night. His mother insisted on fancy dinner napkins at dinner time, and lunch napkins at lunch time. Everyone had to have a full place setting, including a teaspoon, even if they didn't need it. And a knife too, even if there was nothing served that needed cutting. He didn't get it. And the manners. Geez, he thought, if you put your elbows on the table you get whacked with the heel of a knife. Maybe that's why there has to be a full place setting.

When he got back to the dining room, Nick's father had disappeared. Relieved, Nick quickly set the table. He called into the kitchen. "Mom, how much longer until dinner?"

"About three minutes."

"I'll be right back in." Nick slipped out the front door to take a quick look at his bicycle before he sat down to dinner, so he could speak intelligently about the damage to his father. Any cost estimates would be pure guesses, but he wants to be ready to ask for money for a new bike, especially because the old one was too small anyway.

When Nick came back in the front door, he found his father in the foyer standing right in front of him. "Call your brother to the table." Norman turned and went into the dining room.

Sarcastically. Nick obliged. "Rick, dinner!" he yelled.

"I could have done that, you little shit." Nick heard his father mutter from his chair at the table.

"Why didn't you?" As soon as he said it, Nick wished he hadn't. That isn't going to help my cause, he thought. He sighed and joined his father at the table, just as his mother placed the last steaming dish of food on the table.

Nick's brother Rick came stumbling down the stairs and was in his seat at the dining room table before Norman had a chance to respond to his older son. Sheila Lefton backed her way into the dining room through the swinging door from the kitchen, carrying a large carving tray piled high with some kind of overcooked meat. She carefully placed the platter in front of her husband of twenty years.

"What the hell is this?" Norman was weary. His wife was a lousy cook who tended to turn even the finest cut of beef in to a pile of shoe leather.

"It's a rib roast. The ribs are underneath the meat," Sheila answered as she took her seat at the opposite end of the table. "Why?"

"You burned it so far beyond recognition, I had to ask." Norman picked up the serving fork and plunged it into the pile of well-done meat. "All these years I've been eating this crap. Just once I'd like a fat slab of medium rare roast beef, just the way I like it."

"Then go out to Victoria Station." Sheila picked up the bowl of green beans and passed it around to Nick.

Nick had a sinking feeling in his gut. Although he preferred his meat well done, and this was his favorite meal all the way around, it didn't help his cause that his father was in an agitated mood. He had already gotten on his father's bad side by sassing him. He picked up his fork and played with the food on his plate while he tried to figure out a way to broach the subject of a new bike.

Rick, on the other hand, was yammering on and on about his role in the school play. He was stuffing food in his face and talking with his mouth full, and almost singing as he spoke. This, too, worked against Nick's agenda, so he spoke up. "Rick, do you mind? Stop talking with your mouth full. In fact, stop talking altogether and let us eat in peace for once."

"Excuuuuuse me." Rick did not mask his effeminate side. Although he hadn't 'come out' to his family, Nick was sure his brother was gay. His parents were oblivious. It was the late 70's and nobody really talked about it much. Nick wasn't even sure his brother was aware of his own sexuality.

The only sound that could be heard for the next few minutes was the clacking of silverware and an occasional belch, followed by Sheila requesting the obligatory social convention. Finally, after the appropriate amount of time, Nick worked up the nerve to divulge the details of his afternoon mishap and prevail upon his dad for help in replacing his bike.

It didn't go as expected. "How about this?" began Norman. "How about you get yourself a real job, and earn some real money? If you do that, I will give you not enough money for a new bicycle, but for a car!" Norman sat back in his chair, folding his arms on his chest to wait for a response.

Nick dropped his fork. "Did I hear you correctly?" He stared down his father, waiting for the punchline. His dad had always been so frugal, especially where he and his brother were concerned. Nick sat waiting, feeling the almost palpable protestations of his brother.

"You're old enough to take that responsibility on. I'll give you the down payment and add you to our insurance policy. You make the subsequent car payments." Norman looked directly at his son. "That's my offer. No money for a bicycle."

Nick was dumbfounded. Speechless. He didn't have any idea how to proceed. Questions spun in his head. *What kind of job? When would he get the car? What kind of car? How would he juggle school and a job? Boy, a car would really impress Jeanie. How would he get to work unless he got the car first? Should he get a sports car or a practical car? What's Jeanie's favorite color? He should definitely get the car in that color. Would Dad do the same for Rick? Rick is such an ass sometimes.*

"Well? What do you have to say for yourself?" Norman Lefton was nothing if he wasn't a narcissist. This endeavor was more about getting a reaction from his son than anything else.

"I don't know what to say, Dad. I'm so surprised. I only wanted a new bike. I never imagined you would buy me a car." Nick's words were tremulous, spoken softly and carefully. He still was waiting for the other shoe to drop. "I thought for sure you were kidding around."

"Well, I'm perfectly serious. Its time you take on a little responsibility instead of tooling around on that bike of yours every afternoon, accomplishing absolutely nothing. When there's no band practice, you are doing absolutely nothing with yourself. Except maybe drooling over that girl." Norman picked up the serving piece for the roast, paused and with the enthusiasm of a slug, pushed the tongs of the fork into the least cooked slice on the plate. "Geez, Sheila, can't you ever prepare the roast for human consumption?"

"I don't even know where to start looking for a real job. I mean, I won't earn any real money bagging groceries." Nick was picking at the food on his plate, his mind wandering.

"Why don't you see if the music store at the mall needs any help?" offered Rick. "At least it would be something you know about and like."

"Not bad, asshole. Maybe there is a brain in there." Nick scrunched his face up and stuck out his tongue in the direction of his younger brother. He then stuffed a forkful of mashed potatoes into his mouth.

"Nick, really. Please watch your language." Sheila knew it was fruitless to even attempt to stop her boys from name-calling. She had come to accept that this was how they showed each other their love.

Nick reacted in his usual way. "Sooorrrry, mom." Nick could hardly contain himself. He jammed forkful after forkful of his dinner into his mouth barely chewing before he cleaned his plate. "Hey Dad, can we go look for the car after dinner?"

"The dealerships will be closed. I'll take you on Saturday." Norman hadn't bought a new car in years. He was still driving his '58 Plymouth. He was never one to buy the latest car. If it got him where he had to go safely, that was all that mattered. He always took meticulous care of the car inside and out which was why it still ran so well twenty years later. "Any idea what you want to look at? No sportscar, by the way. I'm not paying for that kind of insurance. You can get a nice respectable sedan that looks sporty."

"Ya know what Dad? I've never even thought about it before." Nick actually laughed and smiled at his father. The whole circumstance seemed surreal to him, so it he wasn't the least bit stunned by his reaction by this time. "I guess I'll pay more attention to the car ads on TV between now and Saturday."

"You know, you could read the Herald once in a while, too." Norman smirked at his son, as he put his fork down on his plate. "Any dessert tonight, Sheil?"

"Sorry, I didn't have time to bake anything. I have some cookies."

"Oreos?"

"No, the store brand."

"Oh, never mind." Norman was the one who kept the food budget so tight, yet he was the one who complained the most about what Sheila kept in the house. He pushed back his chair with his legs, while at the same time picking up his plate and glass. He silently carried his dishes in the kitchen and finally yelled over his shoulder, "I'll be in my study."

CHAPTER 4

Nick awoke at 6:16 am on Saturday morning. He rolled over and glanced at his new digital clock radio and thought to himself that he really didn't need to know the exact minute he awoke. This was especially true if he woke in the middle of the night for some reason and the bright red numbers on the clock were glaring 2:47 at him on the night before a big test.

His morning routine on school days was to set his alarm for 6:30 and then hit the 5-minute snooze alarm a minimum of three times before he finally rolled out of bed, throw some clothes on, grab an instant breakfast and hop on his bike in time to make it for roll call at school at 7:10 am. On this Saturday, however, he was going car shopping for his chick magnet. He jumped up and headed for the small bathroom that he shared with his brother. He pushed his shoulder against it fully expecting it to swing open. The pushback jarred him. Reaching down for the doorknob he half-whispered, half yelled, "Rick, what are you doing in there this early?"

Silence. He tried to turn the knob again. It was locked. Nick rapped softly on the door. "Rick, are you in there?"

"I'll be out in a minute. Cool your jets." Rick called back, in a not so early Saturday morning voice.

"Shhhh. You'll wake up the bears." Nick turned on his heels and went back into his bedroom. He grabbed his jeans off the bedpost and slipped them on. Then he rooted through the pile of clothes on the floor for the least wrinkled, least stained t-shirt. Having had little success, Nick resigned himself to wearing a clean shirt from his dresser. He usually reserved those for school. He spoke aloud, to himself. "I wonder if mom is doing laundry today?"

Just as he got his arms through the sleeves and pulled the shirt over his head, Rick poked his head in the door. "It's all yours."

"Who were you in there with, Mrs. Thumb and her four lovely daughters?" Nick was being as sarcastic as possible.

Rick very slowly rolled up the middle finger of his right hand and then violently shook his whole arm and hand at his older brother. "Fuck you."

"Oh now, Ricky, you know mom doesn't like us to use bad words." There was something very rewarding about tormenting a younger sibling. It was, to Nick, almost a rite of passage. "Go back to bed."

Rick had no energy to fight yet another battle with Nick, so he swiveled around and headed back across the dim hallway to his room, pushed open his door and took one last shot at his brother. "I hope you get a lemon."

"Yellow is not my color. I'm an autumn." Nick tossed his head back, mocking his brother's closet sexuality. He laughed out loud at him and then continued into the bathroom.

* * * *

Norman was already downstairs and seated at the dining room table. He had finished off his third cup of coffee and the entire Miami Herald by the time Nick had made his way down the stairs. That in no way is a commentary on Nick's lack of enthusiasm or haste in preparing for the day. Norman was an early riser his entire life, since his days in the military. A lot of his idiosyncrasies can be traced back to his army days: his discipline, his routines, and mostly his demand for respect.

"Mornin, Pops. What's happenin?" Nick had already been to the kitchen and was awkwardly carrying an empty bowl, a box of cereal, a gallon of milk and a spoon. He dumped everything down at the opposite end of the table, waiting for a response from his father. "Dad?"

"I've already scanned the papers for the car dealerships. First I want to know what you have in mind so I can shoot it down before we even leave." Norman was serious. He didn't like arguing in the car while he was driving, nor did he like the push back he always got from his sons on conclusions he has already reached.

"Geez." Nick slumped down into his chair, and slowly prepared his cereal. "You're gonna suck the fun out of this too, arncha Dad?" He picked up the gallon jug of milk and splashed some into his bowl.

"Do you want the car or don't you?" Norman flipped the pages of the car section and opened it up to the Chevrolet page. "Look, here's a Chevy Nova I wanna look at."

"Ugh, that's on old lady car. Can we look at a Camaro?" Nick stuffed a spoonful of a Corn Flakes into his mouth and continued talking. "I really don't want to drive around in a nerd mobile. The Camaro is a hot car."

"Look, you're driving this car to school and to work. Who cares what it looks like?" He turned the page over. "We can look at the Fords too. The dealership is only a few blocks away from Chevy." Norman perused the page, waiting for his son's response.

"Cool, I could get a Mustang."

"Cool, no you can't. Eat your cereal."

"What about a Pinto?" It was clear Norman was looking at price points and practicality and Nick was more interested in style and magnetism.

"Ya know what, Dad?" Nick stood and picked up his bowl. "Let's just go and see what's out there." *Maybe he'll soften when we get there. Maybe he'll recover his virility when he sits in the leather seat of a 1973 Ford*

Mustang. He carried his breakfast paraphernalia back into the kitchen.

"We'll leave in about an hour. The dealerships don't open until 9:00." Norman folded the auto section of the paper and stood up. "I have to see a man about a horse before we go anyway." He headed down the hallway to the guest bathroom and slammed the door behind him.

"Ick." Nick finished rinsing his bowl and spoon and put them down in the sink. He turned on his heels and went out the back door of the kitchen past the guest bathroom door, calling into his father, "I'll be upstairs. Just call me when you're ready to leave." He headed up the stairs, and into his room, slamming the door behind him. Once inside, Nick plopped down on his bed, brooding. *I'm gonna end up with a shit car, if I leave it up to him. I have to find a way to romance him into a sports car. Just get him into the seat of one and paint a picture for him.*

Nick's attention turned to the picture on his night stand. *Jeanie. How can I get you in the back seat of a Pinto or a Nova? Geez, I don't even have the nerve to ask you out, let alone make a move on you. God, you're beautiful. I wish I could ...*

Nick laid back on his bed, resting his head on his pillow, facing the night stand. He unzipped his pants and slipped his hand down inside his underwear. This was always his go-to activity when he had a few minutes to kill. Jeanie's picture stared back at him and in his head, spoke to him. That was why he was always able to achieve an erection so quickly. He didn't know every sixteen-year-old boy could get a hard on in a split second. Being a very private person, he hadn't yet experienced the public embarrassment of a bulge pressing hard against his pants just when a teacher called him up to the chalkboard to figure out a problem in math class.

Oh yeah, oh... you're so hot... oh.... Oh... oh... here I come.... Oh yeah... oh god... oh Jeanie suck me... oh... aahhhhhh.

Nick fell back against his pillow, out of breath. His heart was pounding quickly but faintly in his throat, his forehead moist with sweat. As his body cooled, he slowly came back to the reality that he now had to change both his underwear and his jeans. He unfolded his fingers from his penis and slid his hand from his pants. He jumped up from the bed, wiping his hand on his clothes as he wriggled out of them. Bottomless, he stepped over to his bedroom door to listen for any sound of any family member stirring upstairs. Hearing none, he stuffed the offending clothes in his hamper, grabbed yesterday's underwear from the floor next to it and slid them on. His pants from yesterday were too messed up from the bike accident to wear again, so he opened the dresser drawer and pulled out a pair of shorts. *I'll have to explain this, but dad's clueless, so...*

As Nick zipped up his shorts, he heard Norman calling from downstairs. Let's go, chump." Nick grimaced at the sound of his father's words. *He can't just call me by name. He can't just be nice to me, ever.* Looking directly into the mirror above his dresser, Nick picked up his comb. Mindlessly, Nick ran the comb through his greasy hair as he stared at his face. Puberty hadn't been kind to him. His acne was at its worst on this particular Saturday morning. Bulbous, angry boils on his cheeks and what looked like pink bubble packing across his forehead made him shrink away from the mirror. *It's no wonder Jeanie isn't interested in me. I look like a fucking monster.*

"Coming dad," Nick yelled. He tossed the comb back on the dresser and turned to leave his room. He took one last glance back to be sure he didn't leave any evidence around to reveal his dirty little secret. *Mom won't come in here. She won't do my laundry unless I bring it downstairs. Had that fight last week.* "On my way."

* * * * *

It ended up being a fucking used car. He told me in front of everyone he was buying me a god damned new car. Nick slammed the door shut behind him, kicked his feet up in the air and threw himself on the bed. Staring at the ceiling he crossed his arms in a pout. *What the hell was that all about? A '68 Olds Cutlass Convertible? I was looking at new cars. I had my heart set on a brand new '73 Chevy Camaro.*

Nick got up off the bed and walked over to the dresser. He looked at himself in the mirror. "It's a really cool car, ya know. I mean it will definitely impress the girls. And the car geeks will like it." He picked up the comb and ran it through his greasy hair. His acne was still very angry that afternoon, just like him. He turned away, and headed downstairs for dinner.

Chapter 5

"Who's that kid whose been riding his bike up and down the street in front of the house, Jean. He's kind of creepy." Pat called to his daughter as he wiped the remaining shaving cream from his face, knowing his daughter's bedroom door was open.

Patrick Pearlman was a straight forward guy. His little girl was the only thing that mattered to him in this world since his wife died last year. He saw his role as mother, father, teacher, protector, and whatever else she needed. Jean was getting to an age that made Pat very uncomfortable.

"He's just some guy from school, Dad. I barely know him. I think he has a crush on me." Jeanie called softly from her bedroom. "It means nothing."

Unexpectedly, Pat was standing in her doorway. "Then please ask him to stop."

As suddenly as he was there, he was gone. Jeanie had barely looked up to respond and he was no longer standing there. "Dad, you can't just make a pronouncement and then disappear." Jean scrambled to her feet and scooted over to the doorway. "He's harmless."

"Tell him anyway." Again, Pat was standing back in the hallway, facing his daughter while he buttoned his shirt. "I don't like the fact that he is almost stalking you and that it happens during the afternoons when I'm not even home to protect you."

"All right, Dad, I just don't want to hurt his feelings. I'll tell him."

"Good." Pat returned to his room to finish dressing. "I'm meeting with a real estate agent today honey. With your sister gone, and you leaving in the fall, I'm going to see about selling the house and getting myself a condo closer to downtown."

"WHAAAAT?" In a split second, Jeanie was back at her father's bedroom door. "Daddy you can't sell the house and move. All of our friends live here. All of your support system is in and around this neighborhood. Your golf buddies, the club,

EVERYTHING. You can't move." Julie could feel the blood rushing up the back of her neck, pulsating at the base of her skull. "Where will we all get together for holidays? Where do we come for school breaks? I don't think you've thought the whole thing through."

"I have, honey." Patrick Robert Pearlman never did anything without thinking it through. His history taught him the being impetuous and impulsive didn't work well for him. "I'm not going to live in a studio apartment. It will be a nice sized two-bedroom place, suitable for entertaining, with plenty of room for you and Tina to come home for holidays. I'm even going to have a home office." Patrick spoke calmly and slowly, his words carefully selected. He knew his younger daughter was passionate and emotional, and he was certainly not going to start a war of words this particular morning. His Sunday mornings were reserved for quiet solitude, reading the Sunday paper and devouring a pot of black coffee.

"I sure hope you're making the right decision, Daddy. You know I worry about you." Jean poked her head in the bathroom on her way down to the kitchen. "Can I fix you something for breakfast?"

"No thanks, sweetie. You know my Sunday routine."

"Okay, well I'm going to grab something and then I'm going over to Annette's house. We're having a study group this morning and then we're all going to the beach this afternoon." She stopped herself. "Did you need me for anything today?" She popped a couple of pieces of dry white bread into the toaster and forced the slider down, thinking to herself that it was time to replace the old antique.

"The day is yours. I am expecting you for dinner, though."

"Of course, Daddy. I never miss Sunday dinner." Jean forced the slider back up to retrieve her breakfast. She took a bite of one piece of the dry toast and decided to break from her diet and add some jelly. Spinning around, she faced the refrigerator and found herself eye to eye with the sign she had hung there on New Year's Day: *Every Calorie Counts*. "Well, maybe not." She grabbed her purse that had been hanging over the kitchen chair since the prior evening and stole out the kitchen door.

Once outside, Jean realized that the beach might not be an option. March is a funny month in South Florida. It can either be part of winter, where it's cloudy and the temperature can stay in the low 70's, or it can be part of summer, where it's sunny, hot and humid. Knowing that she had a sweater in the car, Jean moved toward the garage.

Her car, a gift from her parents on her 17th birthday, was a bittersweet reminder to her of her mother, because it was her mother that fought her Dad for it. Letty Pearlman was somewhat of a women's rights activist before it was a true movement. She clashed with Pat for weeks, using some of the language of Gloria Steinem and other female champions of the day. Every time Jeanie put her key in the lock to open the door, she would both gain a sense of competence and yet feel the loss of her mother's perpetual support.

Jeanie tossed her purse across on the front seat and plopped into the driver seat. She turned the key in the ignition, and then reached immediately for the radio knob. Always tuned to Y-100, she turned up the volume to bend her eardrums. Another Carole King song was gracing the airwaves. She already knew all the words and was singing along as she shifted into reverse and began backing up. When she turned her head and stretched her arm around the passenger seat, she noticed a car driving very slowly past her driveway. It was a robin's egg blue convertible. She couldn't tell the make and model, but it was going pretty slow. By the time she had finished backing up the length of the driveway, the car was gone. "That was weird," she said aloud.

Jeanie parked her car on the street in front of Annette's house. She was late, and there was no room left in the circular driveway. It didn't matter, because Annette lived in a posh area and being on a cul-de-sac, she figured her car would be safe. She stood on the marble doorstep, having pushed the doorbell button, and waited. Suddenly the intercom started crackling. "Come in, its open. And come right up to my room."

Jeanie skipped up the winding staircase. Annette's bedroom was just to the right at the top. She elbowed open the door and shouted, "Hey, what's going on in here?"

"Nice to see you too!" Annette laughed. "We started without you... gossiping, I mean. Did you know that Joe Ungar is going out with Margaret Gasper?" Annette lit a cigarette, but started coughing immediately. "I don't know why people like doing this. I don't." She promptly snubbed out the cigarette.

"Really?" Jeanie asked. She tried to hide her disappointment. She had been nursing a major crush on Joe for the past three years, but couldn't get his attention for anything. She had tried everything short of flashing him. "How nice for them."

"Who are you going to ask to the Sadie Hawkins Day Dance?" Annette was being malicious, because she knew damn well that Jeanie had planned on asking Joe. "I'm asking Gary Shapiro."

"EEEEEWWWW! Why would you ask him? He's so gross." Kelly Stein was one of Annette's sycophants.

"It's a joke. Geeeez. How stupid are you?" Annette had no patience for Kelly.

"I haven't really thought about it. I may not go." Jeanie tried again to make light of the whole conversation. She knew she had to tread lightly with her friend Annette. Annette couldn't keep secrets and loved to create chaos among their social circles. She could have any boy she wanted, and she could manipulate the boys in and out relationships with a wink.

"Why don't you ask that Nick guy? Everyone knows he likes you." Annette smirked. Her demeanor spoke volumes. It was Chapter One of yet another volume in the continuing series of 'The Nasty Tales of Annette the Bitch.'

Jeanie shrunk away from the comment, trying to lose herself in her book bag, acting as if she hadn't heard the question.

"Well?" Annette persisted. "Why don't you?"

"Why don't I what?"

"Ask Nick the pizza face to the Sadie Hawkins Day Dance?" Annette snickered. She always found a way to make things exponentially worse with each comment. "Hey, maybe you can ride on the handlebars of his Schwinn."

"You know what Annette? Cut it out. You are such a bitch. Maybe I will ask him. You know, he can't help his acne. You are so mean." Jeanie started re-packing her book bag. "Call me with whatever assignment you want me to do for the project. I'm not gonna sit here and listen to this petty cruelty." Jeanie turned and left the room as abruptly as she had entered.

She tripped her way down the stairs then seized the front door handle and paused. She was sure Annette would come after her, but there was silence. She waited a few more seconds, and the only thing she heard was the slight sound of sinister giggling, echoing from upstairs. She yanked the door open and let it slam behind her as she stomped to her car. As she yanked the door open this time, she thought of her mother in a different way. She thought of how proud her mother would be of her, for standing up for another human being.

Chapter 6

"Quiet down, quiet down." Substitute teachers were never successful in maintaining any kind of decorum in a homeroom classroom at Nick's school. He laughed out loud because the lady who was charged with this responsibility was really suffering this particular Monday morning. *Give it up lady. Nobody gives a shit about the principal's announcements. Unless he's telling us that we can all go home, nobody is going to shut up and listen.*

"Ladies and gentlemen. This is your principal with this morning's announcements. The tennis team won its match against Beach High yesterday, breaking their undefeated run. The golf team came in second in their tournament. There will be a meeting of the Sadie Hawkins Day Dance Committee today after school in Room 224. Ladies, I'm still available if you haven't asked anyone. Let's make this a great event. The lunch ladies have asked me to tell you that today's menu includes a choice: Sloppy Joe's, turkey and gravy with mashed potatoes, and the alternate is macaroni and cheese. That's all for today, and while you're here today, please take the time to.... Learn something."

What a jerk. As if any girl in this school would ask him to a dance. They'd ask ME before they'd ask him and ain't nobody asking me. Maybe there's a wrestling match on that night. Nick found himself doodling all over the back cover of his calculus textbook which was wrapped in that familiar brown grocery bag paper. His mother wasn't necessarily cheap. She was just resourceful. At least that's what she always tells him. When he looked down at his scribbles, he realized that he had been writing Jeanie's name all over the paper. *SHIT! Now I have to do something to cover that up before anybody sees it. Glad I did it on the back at least.*

"Mr. Lefton, the bell rang two minutes ago. Don't you have a class to attend?" The substitute teacher, whose name Nick could not recall, was standing directly over him as he furiously tried to scribble over his previous doodles.

"My class is in this room, ma'am. I don't need to go anywhere." Nick spoke without emotion.

"Oh, okay, then I have you in the next class. I recall that you are a pretty good math student." The sub was recovering from her addled state having survived home room, and was making every attempt to develop an affable relationship with at least one student. "Do you have an idea of what you'd like to pursue after high school?"

Again, a short answer. "Haven't decided." *Leave me alone, will ya?*

"With your aptitude you could go into medicine, science, computers... oh you would be great in physics or computer programming. Have you taken the computer class here at the school?"

"No. With all due respect, ma'am... I'm trying to get some homework done before class. I can't talk right now." *And shut the hell up lady. I don't want to be your friend.* Nick returned to what he was doing.

"I'm sorry. I didn't mean to disturb you. I really thought you were just kind of doodling around. I need to prepare for class anyway." The teacher returned to the front of the room and began writing some equations on the blackboard.

How am I gonna go about asking Jeanie to the dance? I need a fucking miracle to clear up this face of mine before she'll even look at me. She probably already asked somebody anyway. Nick slumped down in his chair, daydreaming, while continuing to scribble across the back of his book. He was shortly interrupted by the trickling entry of his classmates. Some were laughing and talking with each other, but the rest were quietly shuffling in and slumping into their seats. Nobody was paying any attention to the substitute who was trying to maintain some sense of classroom decorum, to no avail.

"Quiet down and take your seats, please. I know this looks like another free class because I'm not your regular math teacher, but trust me, I don't put up with that garbage." Trying to both look and sound tough, the diminutive teacher crossed around to the front of her desk and leaned against it. "I'll wait."

From the back of the room came a muffled, deep voice, "You do that, honey."

None of the other students reacted. They were inured to Telsky's antics. Jimmy Telsky was known around the whole school for giving every substitute trouble. He had even been suspended several times for doing it. There were times when Nick wished he had the guts to join in, because Telsky was funny. But, Telsky had just returned from a three-day suspension that came with a warning that if he did it again, he would be expelled. Nobody knew what "it" was. Everybody knew he smoked cigarettes and dope. Everybody knew he fooled around with girls in his car in the parking lot. Everybody knew he cheated on tests. But nobody knew why he got suspended the last time, nor why he is on probation for expulsion.

"Who said that?" asked the teacher.

Crickets.

"Let me put it another way. Who knows who said that?"

Still, nobody reacted. Nobody even dared to move. Telsky, while very popular, was also known to be a bully. Someone once told Nick that he even had a gun. The class sat in silence, and like Nick, were probably thinking of the consequences of squealing on him.

"Well, that's one way to get you quiet." The teacher stood back up and walked around to the chalkboard. "Mr. Telsky, would you please join me at the board."

She knows everything she needs to know about him. That's pretty funny in itself. Nick sat back in his chair to watch the show.

"Okay, but I ain't good at math." Telsky got up from his seat in the back and hand slapped everyone on his way up the aisle to the front of the room.

"That's why I'm here. It's my job to teach you math. I'll let your English teacher worry about the word ain't." The teacher had her back to the class when she delivered this counter to his sass. The rest of the class reacted accordingly. Some snickered quietly, while others could not hold back outright laughter.

Telsky's face reddened and he turned swiftly to try to catch someone it the act of laughing at him. By then, the room was, once again, silent. His face revealed his anger in no uncertain terms. This was an omen. This was a clear indication that there was going to be a battle to be the first out the door when class was over.

Nick glanced at the clock. Forty-five minutes to go. He knew he had to stay out of Telsky's way the rest of the day. The last time something like this happened, Telsky had beaten him up after school. He tried to concentrate on class, on math, on learning, on everything else but Telsky. He started doodling Jeanie's name, again.

The time passed faster than anyone thought. The bell startled everyone... some from sleep, some from actual interaction with this unique substitute teacher, who had been able to maintain control of the class and impart knowledge.

The rush for the door was as expected. Nick had noticed that most every classmate had already packed up their book bags and backpacks five minutes prior to the time expiring. He ended up being at the end of the line to leave the room. He turned to the teacher and noticed that she was watching the class leave. "Thanks," he offered, half-heartedly.

"You're quite welcome. Have a good day." She added, "Don't back down from him. Don't let anyone keep you from doing the right thing or doing what you want to do."

Nick cocked his head to the side. Her comment had left him pensive, if anything. As the door closed behind him, Telsky was right in his face. "You and me? We'll talk later."

Nick's stomach was in his throat. His backpack slid from his shoulder to the floor, in shock, as if it understood Telsky's words and intent. He bent over to pick it up, trying desperately to think of a plan that takes him out of school a different way than his usual to avoid "talking later" to Telsky. The only thing that came to mind was leaving at that very moment. *No, I'm not a chicken. I'm not gonna let that asshole scare me or keep me from doing what I need to do. Besides. I need to be around Jeanie as much as possible...*

He started down the hall toward his chemistry class. His only source of solace was that Telsky wasn't in any more of his classes the rest of the day. He still can't figure out why he's in the same math class, unless he's just one of those guys who is good at math but doesn't apply himself.

* * * * *

Typical of the afternoons in May in south Florida, the rain was coming down in sheets. Nick couldn't remember if he had put the top up on his car. He stood under the overhang near the back entrance of the school, trying desperately to focus on the student parking lot which was just across the street. He couldn't see twenty feet in front of him for the rain. As usual though, the storm moved quickly and was over as fast as it had started. He laughed out loud at the thought of what his Dad always says about living in Miami. "If you don't like the weather, wait five minutes."

As he stepped off the pavement onto the grass, a shortcut to the parking lot, he realized that it had been raining a lot longer than he knew. He found himself slogging through mud and a few inches of water. The bottoms of his jean legs were both soaked and drawing water up his toward his calves. Suddenly he was thrown to the ground from behind, face down into the water.

"Sucker. What'd you say to her after I left." Telsky had placed Nick in a wrestling hold, jamming his face in the mud while locking his arms behind his head. The backpack sat next to them, also soaking up water.

"Nothing." Nick was trying to talk into the ground. "Just thank you, that's all."

"Thanks for what? For making a fool of me?" Telsky tightened his hold on Nick.

"For teaching. For teaching. That's all."

Telsky pushed Nick's face in the mud one more time for good measure, and then climbed off of him. "Get up, you ass kisser." Telsky stepped back and looked at Nick, standing there covered with mud and soaked. "You better stay in line if you know what's good for you."

Nick said nothing. He turned to walk to the parking lot.

"Did you hear what I said ass kisser?"

Nick kept walking.

"Hey, I'm talking to you." Telsky started following Nick.

Nick spun around suddenly, surprising his predator. "I heard you. But you are not here to boss me around. I am not a rat, nor am I an ass kisser. And I can beat that crap out of you in a fair fight so stop messing with me if you know what's good for YOU." Nick turned back toward the parking lot and stomped away, praying that what he had done had worked. He heard nothing, but he waited until he reached his car to dare to turn his head.

He put the key in the driver's side and finally got the nerve to glance around him. There was no sign of Telsky or anyone else for that matter. The skies were still threatening, so he left the top up, which he had gratefully done that morning. When he finally had gotten himself situated in the driver's seat with the door closed, he sighed heavily, almost breaking down into tears.

The drive home was uncomfortable, Nick's front covered with mud, his jeans soaked. His thoughts turned to Jeanie, as they did most days as he drove home. Having an erection against cold wet underwear and heavy denim was actually unpleasant. He interrupted his thinking suddenly realizing that he had to get home and change his clothes before going to work.

His foot pushed further down on the gas pedal once he was out on the main drag, and since it was only Wednesday, and school lets out early, the rush hour traffic hadn't started yet. Nick's house was only two miles from school, but there were times when it could take twenty minutes to get home.

Nick pulled into the driveway and jumped out of the car. The rain had started to drop intermittently, so he left his backpack on the front seat of his car, not wanting it to get any wetter. It didn't dawn on him that it should be emptied out so everything had a chance to dry out. Seventeen-year-old boys in a hurry didn't think that way.

"Mom, are you here?" Nick shouted to his mother as he skipped up the steps to his room. He hadn't noticed whether her car was down the driveway or not. He never paid attention to her work schedule. There was no response. *Great. Now I can rinse these out and hang them in the shower and then I don't have to deal with dad about fighting.*

Nick was in and out of the house in less than five minutes, and on his way to work. He made his usual detour past Jeanie's house to try to catch a glimpse, but nobody was around. He had been meticulous about planning out where to look for a job, making sure it was somewhere near her house so he could swing by on the way to and or from work.

One of these days, I'm gonna get up the nerve to stop, even if it's to show her my new car. I have to come up with some reason to be there. I'm going to see if I can get a second job delivering pizza or something. Then I can be out and around at night too. What I really need to do is get to her before she asks somebody else to that frickin dance.

Chapter 7

"There's only a week left before the dance, ya know, Jeanie." Annette was acting like her usual snarky self. "You better ask somebody soon or there won't be anybody good left to ask."

"I'm fine, Annette. I know who I'm asking and I'm doing it at lunch today." Jeanie fiddled with her Bic pen, half-doodling half-spinning it on the desk. Her English teacher had not come into the classroom, allowing everyone plenty of time for gossip. The boys were sparring, talking sports and flirting. The girls were in their usual cliques, sizing each other up, whispering and giggling and the loners were sitting quietly either reading or daydreaming.

"Just saying that you never know who might have asked whom already."

"Perfect use of the English language." Ms. Jordan announced as she walked in the door. Annette's voice apparently had reached the front of the room. "Who knows why I said that?"

Jeanie raised her hand.

"Jeanie, let someone else answer for a change. How about you, Barbara?"

Barbara Hurst was one of those 'loners' sitting in the back of the room, and hadn't been paying attention. "The bell hasn't rung so I wasn't listening yet."

"Fair enough. Who was listening?" Ms. Jordan glanced around the room to find nobody raising their hand. She reluctantly returned to Jeanie, nodding to her. "Well?"

"She said WHO might have asked WHOM instead of WHO."

"Correct." Ms. Jordan pulled her chair out and sat down at her desk and opened up her attendance book. After calling out all of the names of her students and marking the book she closed it and put it in the top drawer of her desk.

"Let's get right down to it. Let's start with some general statements about To Kill A Mockingbird, and then we'll pick one or two and drill down into it in what I hope, if you guys finished reading it over the weekend like you were supposed to, will be a spirited discussion."

She stood up, picked up a piece of chalk and turned toward the class. "Okay, who is going to start us off?"

Annette raised her hand. "Harper Lee always considered her book to be a simple love story, didn't she?" Nick thought to himself, *ass-kisser*.

"Straight from the Cliff Notes. Not using it, Next?"

Jeanie raised her hand. "I got the feeling it was a study in black and white. You know, opposites. And how we all have that in life, but there's life in between as well."

"Interesting." Ms. Jordan wrote the words 'human behavior-black and white.' She turned back around. "Anyone else?"

Barbara shouted from the back of the room. "It was a simple story of a sleepy Southern town and the crisis of conscience that rocked it. I think it kind of goes together with the first one you wrote, though."

"How so? Let's expand on this." Ms. Jordan paused. She loved this group of kids. No matter how different they were from each other, they were always able to get a great dialogue going around the literature they were asked to read. "Anyone."

Nick slowly raised his hand. He was never a big participant in these discussions. *This might give me a chance to have a way to approach Jeanie after class.* "Well, there were a lot of examples of the extremes. There was innocence versus knowledge, kindness versus meanness, love versus hatred, humor versus sadness. There's probably a lot more but I can't think of it right now."

Ms. Jordan was awestruck. The entire class was silent. Nick could feel his face radiating with heat, knowing that he was blushing. "Amazing! Nick! That is brilliant. Okay, let's use those as topic headers and get into the meat of the story."

English class flew by. Before they knew it, the class was packing up their notebooks and backpacks and moving toward the door. Nick tried to get in front of Jeanie so he could be in the hall when she came through the door. When she did, she actually smiled at him. "Nick, that was great. You really got the class going today."

Nick's chest fluttered. He felt like his heart skipped a beat. "Thanks!" *I think that may be the first word I ever heard Jeanie say directly to me and it was so nice.* "I really liked the book. How about you?" But Jeanie had already gotten lost in the crowded hallway. It didn't matter to Nick. He was making headway, and that's all that mattered to him. He walked lightly down the hall to his next class. *I'll see her at lunchtime and ask her.*

* * * * *

The clatter of silverware and trays always made it unpleasant for Nick to eat lunch in the cafeteria. He never usually stayed inside for lunch. There was a bank of picnic tables right outside the back door of the school, next to the driver's education course. He enjoyed the fresh air, and there was always entertainment watching the sophomores drive for the first time or two. But this day, he was going to grab a table near where Jeanie was sitting, and he was going to buy his lunch, a healthy looking one, to try to impress her.

After getting through the lunch line, Nick made a cursory glance around the cafeteria trying to locate Jeanie's usual lunch bunch. He spotted them in the corner, however Jeanie wasn't with them. Maybe she was in line behind me. *I'll walk slow and maybe she'll pass by.*

Nick stopped and needlessly rearranged things on his tray. That's when he spotted Jeanie at the far end of the cafeteria, diametrically opposed to where all of her friends were sitting. She sat alone at a small table, her tray to the side, her face in her hands with her elbows treacherously close to the edge of the table. Nick took long strides in her direction, balancing his tray with one hand while attempting to pull out a clean but crumpled handkerchief out of his pocket.

"Um, are you all right?" Nick asked tentatively. He could feel his voice shaking as he spoke. "I didn't expect to see you back here."

"I'm okay, thanks." Jeanie didn't look up.

Nick was afraid to push any further, but knew it was now or never. "Crying. Doesn't seem like you're okay." He paused. Not having an option to turn pack, he forged forward. "Is there anything I can do to make it better, whatever it is?" He knew better than to ask exactly what was making her cry. He has been snapped at one too many times. He's been called nosey and nerdy, and has been told to get lost, go away, go fly a kite, go play in traffic and a multitude of other not very nice things. *If she wants to answer me, she will.*

"Why are girls so bitchy to each other? I mean, I don't get it. When you're supposed to be friends, why do they try to hurt you on purpose?"

"I wish I knew the answer."

Jeanie picked her head up and locked eyes with Nick. His stomach churned and his chest was pounding. "You know what Nick? Would you like to be my escort to the Sadie Hawkins Day Dance?"

Nick's knees buckled. *I have absolutely no feeling in my feet. Please don't let me drop my tray.* He put his tray down on the table. "Um, what did you say?"

"I asked Joe Marino to the dance only to find out that Annette had already asked him and he's going with her. Annette KNEW I wanted to ask him. She KNEW I liked him. She's such a bitch." Jeanie dropped her face back into her hands and began sobbing all over again.

Nick shook out the wrinkled linen handkerchief and offered it to Jeanie. "It's clean. I just had it in my pants pocket instead of my shirt. I always get teased for carrying it there."

Jeanie reached out and took it from him. "Thank you." She paused, looking at him thoughtfully. "You know, Nick, you are very sweet."

Nick blushed. "Nah."

"So, would you go with me?" Jeanie looked straight at him this time. Then she sucked the life out him by adding, "as friends?"

Nick fell into the chair beside her. He didn't know how to answer her. He had gotten what he wanted, but not quite how he wanted it. It reminded him of his father's Rule Number One. You can tell someone what to do or how to do it, but not both. *I guess I should be happy I've gotten this far.*

"I would be honored to be your escort... as friends." *Just being considered your friend is a whole lot more than I had when the day started.* "We'll have fun.

Now let's change the subject so we can get those tears to go away. I really enjoyed English class today. How about you?"

Nick and Jeanie talked about Atticus Finch as if they knew him personally as they finished their lunches together. Nick considered this day one of the best of his life.

* * * * *

The weekend came quickly and Nick's nervousness rose exponentially as each day passed. He had gone to work every day after school, knowing full well that every dollar he earned that week would be spent on clothes for the dance and a corsage for Jeanie. He was going to take every opportunity to advance this friendship into more than a second-choice date. He was going to woo her and impress her with his manners and his charisma. He spent hours working on his acne and his hair. He practiced talking to her in front of the mirror, with more failures than successes.

Finally, Friday had come. Nick sat fully dressed and ready on the edge of his bed, staring at the clock on his night table. The dance was called for 7:30 and it was only six. He found himself trying to steady a bouncing knee, licking his parched lips and swallowing hard to wet his dry throat. His gut was tied in knots and his head was pounding. Abruptly jumping to his feet, he began yelling at the mirror. "Stop this. Stop freaking out. This is exactly what you want."

Nick left his room and skipped down the stairs. His father was, as usual, planted at the dining room table, perusing the evening paper. "Hey Dad, ya got a minute?"

Mr. Lefton looked up from the News. "Jeez. Its Friday. The weekend, ya know? I'm off duty until Monday. Why don't you bother your mother?"

Nick dropped his shoulders. He wasn't surprised by his father's reaction, just disappointed. "It's not really something I can talk to Mom about. Kind of a male question."

"Oh, all right. What is it?" Mr. Lefton carefully folded up the section of the paper that he was reading and carefully placed back in the slot from which he had pulled it. He slid his reading glasses off his nose and placed them neatly on top of the paper.

"I'm just nervous about this date tonight. I'm supposedly going as a friend, but I want more out of the relationship. Should I try to kiss her goodnight? Should I slow dance with her close up? I have no idea what to expect."

"If its anything like the Sadie Hawkins Day dances we used to have back in the forties, you all will be on one side of the room and the girls will all be giggling and gossiping on the other side of the room. They'll eventually move the punch bowl table out on the dance floor just to get the Hatfields and the McCoys to at least come together for drinks." He laughed in his son's face as he got up from the table. "You're wasting your time day-dreaming about getting a kiss."

"Thanks for the encouragement, Dad." *What a pain in my ass. I'll kiss her on the cheek and say thank you. Despite what he says, I'm getting a frickin kiss tonight.* Nick turned his back on his father, left the room and then skipped back up the stairs to his bedroom, to wait out the last painful minutes, until he was to leave.

* * * * *

Shit. I can't believe this is happening. She is a knock-out and she asked me to take her tonight. Nick stood in the landing as he watched Jeanie come down the stairs. His heart was thumping so hard he grabbed his chest. *Cut it out, you fag. You're acting like your brother.*

"Hi Nick. Thank you for doing this." Jeanie reached the bottom of the stairs, although she didn't appear to Nick to be very happy. "I guess I just have to make an appearance and then we can leave."

"I am at you service," Nick responded. "Whatever you would like to do is fine with me. I'm just happy to be taking you." *Boy did that sound needy. I have to act like I belong here.*

"Let's get this over with."

"You know, you don't have to go in with that feeling. Let's you and me walk in there like we own the place. Let's act the Queen and King of the prom. Let's just go and dance and have fun."

"You know what?" Jeanie perked up. "You're right! I'll show those snotty girls and stupid guys how to have a have a good time." She grabbed Nick by the arm and hurried him out the door and down the walkway to his car. "Can you put up the roof so my hair doesn't get messed up? We can drive home with it down, because then it won't matter."

And they were off.

* * * * *

"My dad told me it would be like this." Nick tried to make idle conversation, referring to the fact that the teenagers were separated by an imaginary wall, the girls giggling and whispering, the boys sizing up the girls and talking of conquests. "Let's break the ice and get out on the dance floor."

"Can we wait for a fast song. I'm a little uncomfortable dancing slow on the first dance." Jeanie gestured to the deejay to speed it up. He got the message and cued up "Y M C A" by the Village People.

Nick and Jeanie moved out onto the side of the dance floor and began doing the iconic dance and before long many others joined them. Soon they were lost in the crowd. The Deejay continued playing songs that would keep the kids on the dancefloor, to Nick's dismay, as they were all loud and upbeat. He waited endlessly for a slow song, for a chance to finally touch Jeanie.

Nick finally left Jeanie on the dance floor to get something to drink. He stood in front of the punch bowl seething. *What the fuck. This is a waste of time. Shit. Now she's dancing in a line dance with everyone but me.* He turned back to the punch bowl and looked at his reflection in the smooth, glassy top. *It's no wonder. Look at my fucking face.*

The blare of the trumpets and heavy beat of the bass died down, and the familiar smoky, resonant tones of Al Green began, heralding the emptying of the dance floor. Nick dropped his punch cup on the table and pushed his way through the force of bodies leaving the dancefloor to try to find Jeanie. He reached her just as she was approaching the edge of the parquet. "Come on, let's keep this thing going." He grabbed her by the arm and pulled her back on the floor.

While Nick really wanted to touch her, he acted like the perfect gentleman on the dance floor. He was nervous, so he didn't try to move his hands down her back to touch her buttocks. He didn't try to breathe softly in her ear. He didn't do any of the things he had read about. He didn't even pull her close enough to feel her breasts against his chest. While he felt like he missed an opportunity, he still couldn't hide the fact that he had a small erection after the dance. When the song was over, Nick followed close behind her when they exited the dance floor, and offered to get her a cold drink.

The remainder of the dance was uneventful. Jeanie seemed content just to stand and watch, having had her fill of dancing. Nick was strutting around as if he had been the catalyst for all of the festivities of the evening, including all of the girls that would get felt up and all of guys that would get French kissed or even laid that night. After a short while, Jeanie turned to Nick and asked to leave.

This is it. Okay. Just be cool. "If that's what you would like, sure, we can go." Nick took Jeanie by the arm, and without a word, they left the dance.

* * * * *

Nick parked his car on the curb in front of Jeanie's house and jumped out. He ran around the front end as fast as he could to be sure he could open the door for Jeanie before she had a chance to do it herself. She was still gathering her sweater and purse when he grabbed the handle a swung the door open so hard that it bounced back and knocked him over with enough force to throw him into the side of the car.

"Are you okay?"

"Nothing hurt but my pride." Nick reached out his hand to help Jeanie from the passenger seat. She took his hand and stepped out onto the sidewalk. Nick softly shut the door behind her and then escorted her up the sidewalk to the front door in silence.

"Would it be too forward to ask for a kiss goodnight?" Nick was making every attempt to be a gentleman, but this was the pinnacle of his dream date with a girl for whom he had been longing for years.

"I suppose it wouldn't hurt."

Nick stepped close to Jeanie and put his arms around her. He leaned in and put his lips to hers. His mouth abruptly overtook hers, his tongue forcing its way between her lips and foraging around in her mouth like a bear in winter, looking for food. For what was an eternity to Jeanie seemed like a split second to Nick, who pushed further and further into this foray. Jeanie forced her arm up in between them and elbowed Nick in the chest.

"Ow! That hurt!" Nick fell away." What was that for?"

"We were going as friends, Nick. That wasn't just a goodnight kiss." Jeanie turned toward the door. "Do me a favor. Don't ask me for anything again."

"What did I do?"

"You took advantage of the situation. This was not a date, and you know it. You had no business forcing that tongue of yours. Good night."

Jeanie turned and went into the porch, letting the screen door slam behind her. She then slammed the front door after it. Nick stood dumbfounded, his pride hurt and his erection more than noticeable. He dropped his shoulders, turned and sluffed back to his car.

CHAPTER 8

Nick Lefton had stopped relying on an alarm clock. He was a light sleeper these days and when something important was coming up, he was always up early on that day. This day was the first day of senior year. He also didn't want his alarm clock going off and waking up his younger brother. Rick was starting school at the high school as a freshman this year. Nick was in no hurry to be seen with his fairy younger brother. He got picked enough at that school without having a fag for a younger brother.

Without making a sound, Nick got up and dressed and downstairs in less than ten minutes. There was not a peep coming from Rick's room. Nick was almost hoping his brother would be late on his first day. Both his parents were already gone for work, so Nick grabbed a toaster pastry and quietly left the house through the back door. *That damn car of mine is a pain in the ass. I can't believe I have to walk to school on the first day of my senior year. At least the repair wasn't too much this time Fucking car. If Dad had let me get a new car instead of his damn 'classic' car it would still be under warranty.*

Nick started off down the quickest route to school. It meant having to go through a few back yards, but he knew all the neighbors. He probably babysat or cut their lawns at one time or another in the past two or three years. None of the other kids in the neighborhood did stuff like that. They all had real jobs or didn't have to work. He passed by his uncle's house and spit on the sidewalk, there.

"That's disgusting!" A voice came up from behind him at the same time he felt a sharp smack in the back of his head. "Did you think you were pulling one over on me by leaving without me?"

Rick skipped circles around him as Nick tried to continue walking. "Shut up, asshole." Nick kept walking forward. "Walk a different way. We all know you do."

"Fuck off." Rick ran on ahead and disappeared around the next corner.

What a little shit. Actually, he might get beat up if he keeps on with that skipping shit. Nick tried to put his brother out of his mind. His thoughts turned to Jeanie. *I wonder if I'm going to have any classes with her this year... I'm not in her section. She's too smart for me. The only way we'll be together is in homeroom or an elective. Wish I knew what electives she's taking. I'd even take Home Ec if I knew she would be in the class. I wouldn't even care if I got bullied. It would be worth it. I got nothing left to lose.*

Lost in thought, Nick didn't notice that he had come upon the bike racks outside the south end of school. This was the hangout of Telsky and his friends, one of whom had casually slid his leg out just far enough for Nick to trip over. He maintained his footing without falling, but Nick bumped into Telsky, himself.

"Watch it, asshole." Telsky pushed Nick off to another of his bully friends.

"I don't want him." Nick got shoved again.

"Get lost, wimp."

Nick was able to avoid landing on or even near another of Telsky's crew. One thing he knew about these guys is that they were easily weirded out by crazy. Nick gave them the best version of crazy he could, "Get off a me... don't touch me or I'll kill ya... I'll kill everyone a ya... Blaaaaaaaaaahhhhhh." He yelled as he ran down the double sidewalk toward the school.

Telsky yelled after him. "Don't think this is over you prick."

How come every other kid in the whole fucking school can walk by those assholes and not have a problem, but when I come along, I become a beach ball for them? Why do they have to pick on anyone? Nick opened the double doors of the end of the high school. It was the freshman building, but it was a quick walk through. He just wanted to avoid seeing Rick.

Nick walked through the plaza diagonally to the senior building. There were a few familiar faces sitting around talking. There was at least ten minutes before the bell. Nick considered sitting down there to do a "Jeanie watch" as he had come to refer to those times when he would stalk her. He didn't know some people would refer to it as stalking, least of all Jeanie. He thought better of it when he realized Telsky's crew was likely to find him there too.

Entering the building on the north side, Nick scanned the halls for Jeanie but didn't see her so he went on to his homeroom. The bell rang as he slid into seat in the back of the room. He felt a sense of darkness descend down over him. It was going to be a long day. At least he didn't have to move from his seat for his first class.

The day lasted longer than Nick expected. Not only was Jeanie in none of his classes, but she didn't share the same lunch hour, nor did he even see her the entire day. Nick sat at the desk in the back corner of his English Literature Class, his one last hope, waiting for everyone to take their seats, hoping that Jeanie would appear in his last class of the day, but she did not. He spent the last fifty minutes of his first day of senior year daydreaming and doodling all over the class syllabus. He heard nothing the teacher said and was unprepared when she called upon him to answer a question that he did not hear.

"Yes? I'm sorry, can you repeat the question?"

The entire class broke out in a raucous laughter.

"I simply asked you to tell us your name."

The class laughed again, including Telsky, who was seated in the front row. Nick could hear his voice from the front. "Ass wipe."

Nick stood up. "My name is not ass wipe, you piece of cow dung."

"Okay, okay, settle down," The teacher knew immediately she had a war on her hands. "Mr. Telsky, your comments are not necessary nor welcome."

"My name is Nick Lefton, and I apologize. I wasn't paying attention because I have something very important on my mind. It won't happen again."

Class continued without issue. Nick did not participate, but he did pay attention. It was English class where he met Jeanie last year. *If I want to have something in common with her, I need to, at minimum, stay up to speed in this class.*

The bell rang precisely at 3:20 PM. Nick hurled himself for the back door of the classroom, making every attempt to avoid Telsky. His saving grace was that he had to pick up the bus at the Northeast side of the school to get to work. That was the diagonal opposite of where the bike rack was, and where Telsky's gang would meet after school.

Feeling as though he had avoided an altercation, Nick dropped his shoulders, although not in relaxation. He was glad he didn't have to fight, but he was still feeling that sense of doom hanging over him. Just a glimpse of Jeanie would have helped. He walked slowly out to the bus stop and found a seat on the bench.

The wait for bus was more of an annoyance to Nick than anything else. Several younger girls were standing behind the bench tittering about some inanities. There was a man sitting next to him smoking a smelly cigar. There were a few other people milling around. Nick had never noticed how busy this particular bus stop was before.

When the bus pulled up and belched to a halt, everyone who was boarding seemed to crowd the door like ants on a small piece of cookie. Nick tried, too, to be the first. He didn't want to have to stand. When the doors opened three people tried to get off the bus into the group of people waiting to get on.

Nick paused and then climbed the steps. He slowly walked down the aisle, heading toward the back of the bus when, suddenly, the bus driver lurched the bus into gear, knocking him off balance and causing him to fall back into the man behind him.

"Don't say excuse me or anything," said the man, sarcastically.

Without even thinking, Nick backhanded the man. "Why don't you just shut your trap. Better yet, tell the bus driver not to put his fucking foot on the gas until everyone is seated."

The man, twice Nick's age and not very big, was not looking to start anything with an angry hot-headed teenager, so he backed away and watched Nick move ahead and find his seat.

Nick went straight to the back of the bus and dropped his backpack on the window seat and plopped down into the aisle seat. As soon as he did, he changed his mind, stood up and traded places with his bag so he could stare out the window on the way to work. He was in a pensive, thoughtful mood, and he knew he had a few minutes on the bus to think things through.

What the hell is wrong with me? Why did I slap that guy? I'm the one who fell into him. It really wasn't his fault. My life sucks. I'm too stupid for college, too lazy for manual labor and too weak for construction work. Jeanie is going to go away to some fancy school and she'll be around a bunch of fraternity boys. I got nothin. Even that fairy brother of mine is going to do better in life than me.

When his stop came up, Nick dragged his bag through the aisle to the front of the bus. When he came upon the guy he hit, he stopped and offered a meek apology. "Sorry man." He didn't wait for a response. He figured that was more than most teenagers would have done. He laughed to himself picturing Telsky in the same position. *First it would have been calling the guy an ass wipe, I'm sure. He would probably then smack him and walk away, and then turn back and tell him to stay out of his way, like threatening him.*

Nick skipped down the steps of the bus, almost tripping. He had only one block to walk to his job, and since he wanted to keep this one, he found himself power-walking toward the storefront entrance. He knew he was lucky to have the job, because it paid twice the minimum wage, and he was loved being around the auto parts. His boss was a classic car fanatic and loved cars like Nick drove. It was Andy's recommendation to use the mechanic that was fixing his car right now.

"Hi Andy," yelled Nick as he thrust the front door to the store open. "Sorry I'm a minute or two late. The bus was a little off schedule."

"Not to worry, man," came a scratchy voice from the back. Andy was a throwback to the sixties and was still sporting long hair, torn jeans and the distinct odor of stale marijuana. Nick always thought the place smelled like skunk. "I was just finishing up some of your work from yesterday... inventory shit." Nick wasn't sure if he was kidding or not.

"Sorry, I thought I had finished it all."

"You did. The delivery came right after you left." Andy sat on the stool behind the cash register. "I was just pullin wool, man."

"Remember I have to get over to Gary before five today to pick up my car." Nick knew this wasn't a problem, but he also knew he had to remind Andy often. He figured Andy's brain was a little fried from all of the drugs he did.

"Yeah, I got it."

The afternoon went quickly. Andy's business was well-established and very popular among people of all ages, mostly men, and some women. Nick's responsibilities had grown over the summer and besides doing stock, he now was doing customer service and Andy had begun to trust him at the cash register. There were no incidents today, and Nick was ready to clock out at 4:45.

"Nice, smooth day, huh Nicky boy?" Andy returned from the back and took his place at the cash register. "I'll see you tomorrow, man."

Nick walked down the street slowly, his mind wandering back to his homework, Jeanie, Telsky and what he might have to choke down for dinner. Gary's Garage was only two blocks away and he knew that the car would be ready and he had the cash in his pocket, so he didn't feel rushed. He was exhausted. The early school schedule coupled with the anxious night he had the night before left his tired before lunch. Andy had him lifting heavy boxes of auto parts to stock shelves when business was slow. *Can't wait to get home and sleep for a while before dinner.*

The car was, indeed, ready. Gary pocketed the cash, as there was no invoice. Nick hopped in the car, tossing his backpack on the passenger seat. He turned the key, and revving the engine, evoked an explosion. It sounded like someone shot off a roman candle.

"Hey, kid. I told you not to rev the car. The fuel line can't handle it... there's no fuel injection system in that car." Gary yelled from inside the office.

"Oh yeah, I forgot." *Sure does make a cool noise, though.* Nick backed out of the garage parking lot and drove home.

Chapter 9

There was nothing special about the end of school year for Nick. He wasn't going to prom. He was barely going to make it to graduation, having had serious difficulty completing his classwork. He had become overly passionate about his photography elective to the detriment of his required classes. Because of this, he certainly knew he wasn't going off to college for summer session, much less in the fall. The only thing he was focused on now was getting as much time with or around Jeanie as he could. He had weathered his entire senior year without having the benefit of sharing a single class with her, so any interaction had to be planned. He had hoped she would be working on the yearbook, but she dropped out. *And there was no possibility of getting a date with her because of that damn boyfriend of hers, that asshole. He was always around. I couldn't sit with or even near her at lunch.*

"Nicholas Lefton, Ellen Lester, Kelly Letterman, and Alan Loach, please go across to the office to pick up cap and gown." Teachers really didn't care about teaching anything in senior classrooms during the last two weeks of school. Good teachers talked with the kids about where they were headed, what they would study and things like that. This teacher wasn't one of those. Mr. Sanders didn't really care anymore. He was retiring after forty years and just wanted it to be over. He sat back in his desk chair reading the newspaper, waiting for each group of four to return before he sent the next four.

"Is the whole day going to be like this?" Nick tried to strike up a conversation with the two girls with whom he was in line. Neither of the two girls responded. Nick had, by now established himself as the strange kid in the class. His appearance had slipped immeasurably, his hair long a straggly, usually greasy. His clothes were usually stained with auto grease from constant tinkering with his car after work. His reputation, too, for being kind of creepy around girls had gotten around. His antics with Jeanie after the Sadie Hawkins Day dance were well known.

Jeanie had let it slip that he was a little aggressive, and her 'friends' spread the word that he had attacked her.

"I'm not going to bite, ya know." Nick was tired of being ignored. *Bitches. I'd love a minute or two with each one of you alone. I'll show you something to be afraid of.* "Do either of you know if there is anything else planned for classes today?"

Still no answer. Finally, the other boy in their group turned around. "No, Nick. If you have your cap and gown, after this class, you can go home, but there are classes tomorrow."

"Thanks, but I didn't ask you, jerk. I wanted these pretty little ladies to show me a little respect." Nick returned his attention to the two girls. They had moved up further in the line in an attempt to gain distance from Nick. It was clear by their body language that he had gotten under their skin. At the front, the line split off into two: the girls to the left and the boys to the right.

Nick gave up on his current conquest as he spotted Jeanie at the table, picking up her red cap and gown. Just the sight of her made him feel different inside. His chest fluttered and he could feel a tingling in this groin. He wasn't getting erections every time he saw her anymore. The fact that he had collected hundreds of photographs of her over the past year, mostly from a distance, had desensitized him somewhat. He no longer kept his pictures in a file folder in his night stand. He had photo albums, posters and wallets size pictures. He had even turned his closet into a dark room, where he spent all of his free time, developing and printing myriad rolls of film and photographs of his beloved Jeanie. The closet had also become what some may call an eerie gallery, but nobody has seen it, not even his mother. He had put a lock on the door, so she can't even hang up his clothes in there.

Nick scribbled his signature across the line next to his name, grabbed his cap and gown and spun around to try and spot Jeanie. She had already gone. He slowly returned to his classroom and signed out with Mr. Sanders, who never bothered to look up from his newspaper. *What the fuck? You have no idea who the hell is here and who left. Ass hole.*

I don't have to be at work for two hours so what the hell am I supposed to do. Go home? Nah, nothing happening there. I could go across the street to the mall and get something to eat. Nick walked slowly through the hallway toward the back exit to the student parking lot. There were only a few kids in the halls. There was a creepy emptiness in his gut as he pushed open the double doors. His backpack was over one shoulder, his cap and gown over the other, freeing his hands to reach in his back pocket and pull out the crushed pack of Marlboros and a soggy pack of matches. While he wasn't taking great care of himself, he never smoked in his car. He took meticulous care of his baby. The one thing he couldn't get rid of was that annoying backfire. The new cars all come with a fuel injection system, so they don't do that. *Technically, I could have a fix installed, but I really can't afford that.* Nick lit up a cigarette and slowly walked toward the parking lot.

"Hey Ass wipe." Nick knew that voice. Worse, he knew the only person who called him that was Telsky. He didn't turn around or let Telsky know that he had heard him. He took a long drag on his cigarette and kept walking.

"You heard me, you ass wipe. Stop walking or I'll take your legs out from under you, you little shit." Telsky was running up from behind Nick. "I need a ride and you're gonna give it to me."

Nick stopped suddenly, causing Telsky to run right into him. "Ummph. What the hell?" Nick turned around. In the past year, Nick had actually grown taller than Telsky, and had filled out enough to present a decent challenge to his threats. "I'm not going anywhere. I'm just dumping my shit in the car and then going across the street."

"You're not going to work at Andy's place?" Telsky actually showed a shade of disappointment—a sort of vulnerability that Nick had never seen before. "Shit. He has something for me."

"I'm going over to get something to eat at the mall, and then I'm going to work."

"I'll go with you."

"That's a lot to take for granted. Who said I invited you? Why would I want to give you a ride, much less eat with you? You have been a thorn in my side my whole time here at this fucking school." Nick kept walking.

"Hey man, wait up." Telsky followed Nick. "I'm sorry. I won't bully you anymore. I just really need to get over to Andy's place. It's really important." Telsky was humbling himself. "I'll even buy your lunch."

Nick stopped and looked at Telsky. Something was different. He did, indeed, look vulnerable, but Nick couldn't quite figure out why. "What's your problem? You think after four years of beating the crap out of me, and my brother, I'm gonna just accept one I'm sorry?"

"I was messed up. Look, I'm not even graduating. I have to stay back a year if I want a diploma." Telsky stopped talking and looked down. Almost as if it was under his breath, Telsky confided to Nick that he had to get to Andy because Andy had some cocaine for him. He admitted to Nick that he was hooked on it.

"Stupid."

"I know. I have to get off of it but I need some now." Telsky was still staring at his feet. "So, can we go grab a quick sandwich and then go to Andy?"

Nick hesitated for a minute. *I'm not sure I want this guy getting to close to me. And I'm definitely sure I don't want him in my car. But man, he's like really pathetic right now.* "I guess so. Come on."

They walked briskly through the student parking lot and diagonally through the busy intersection to the newly remodeled mall which sat conveniently across the street. Throughout the school year, hundreds of kids would sneak out of school and run rampant through the mall at lunch time, skipping out on checks, shoplifting and wreaking havoc. Mall authorities had posted new requirements that precluded anyone under the age of 18 from entering without an adult. Both Nick and Telsky had crossed the age threshold during the spring and could enter freely. Telsky, however, was banned from several of the stores for various reasons.

"Where do you want to have lunch?" Nick asked.

"The only place I can go is to the food court. I'm not allowed in the department store or the Five and Dime." He was walking with his head down, watching his feet move one in front of the other, seemingly amazed that they were working in concert with each other. "I'm not really hungry, so go where you want, and I'll wait." Telsky had lost a lot of weight in the past few months, having little appetite for food or sleep.

"I'll just grab a sandwich then, because once I get to work, I won't be able to eat till I get home and that won't be till about ten tonight."

"I really don't give a fuck about your dietary schedule. Next thing you're going to chime in about, is your bowel habits. Just get your lunch so we can go."

Hey shithead. I'm the one doing you the favor. Don't be biting my head off. I'll take my own fucking sweet time. You're the ass hole that got yourself fucked up on cocaine. Not me. Nick slowed down his pace to a stroll. The two boys walked through the mall, passing store after store. Nick stopped to look at every other display window, sometimes engaging Telsky in conversation, sometimes just staring, knowing he was driving his companion to extremes.

When they ultimately reached the food court, Nick headed for the deli and ordered a sandwich and drink while Telsky found a table near the exit. Nick came back to the table with his tray, offering half his sandwich and a drink to Telsky, who politely declined. "At least drink something. Its hot out there and we still have to walk back to the parking lot."

Reluctantly, Telsky sipped on the soda while Nick scarfed down his sandwich. There was no conversation. Their eyes never met. Telsky, for all his bullying and tough-guy exterior seemed so small and unthreatening to Nick. Telsky was the only person other than family members with whom Nick had spent more than a minute or two talking in the past year. Even his customer service skills had been suffering as of late and Andy had him in the back doing the books and ordering merchandise.

"Come on, man, finish up!" Telsky stood up and slurped on the last of his drink. Looking around for the nearest trash can, he was visibly agitated. "I really need to go." He stepped to his right and tossed his cup into an open trash can. Shoving his hands deep into his front pockets, Telsky stood, bouncing in his shoes.

"Okay, okay." Nick stood up and picked up his tray and slowly walked over to the trash receptacle. He dumped his trash in the can and placed his tray on the top. "Let's go."

"If we go through this store, it has a back door that lets out to the rear parking lot." Nick started to open the door.

"I'll get chased out. they got my picture up by the register in there."

"There's nobody by the register. We can make a beeline right for the back of the store and nobody will even notice you. Just keep your head down and walk fast." Nick was determined to take the short cut.

"Shit, man. If they catch me, it'll be a whole thing with the Mall security and it'll be that much longer until I can get over to Andy's."

"What are you, a wimp? Come on, big, tough Telsky." Nick had never felt so much power over Telsky and wasn't about to let the opportunity pass him by. "You realize that if you don't do this, it will be all over school tomorrow."

"Yeah, you do that and I'll have your head."

Telsky was never one to back down, so he pushed Nick out of the way and walked head up into the store. He took long, stealthy strides past the counters and displays, and right past the cash register to the narrow hallway that led to the back entrance. Nick followed him like a puppy dog, feeling as though he had accomplished something no other kid in the school had been able to do all year. *I, Nick Lefton, have intimidated Telsky! Behold the great Nick Lefton. All bow to his power and greatness. I reign supreme over the small and insignificant Telsky.*

The two boys found themselves nearly skipping down the steps into the parking lot, and then broke into a run across, dodging occasional parked cars to the street directly in front of the high school. Telsky stopped. He grabbed his chest. "Wait up. I need to catch my breath."

"Fine. I'm not the one in a hurry." Nick stopped, turned around to see Telsky doubled over. He walked back a few feet. "You okay?"

"Just some cramps."

Nick put his hands on his hips, trying to gather his own composure. "Can I help?"

"No, dammit, just leave me alone a minute. I'll be fine."

"Want me to go get the car and come back for you"

"NO! I said I'd be okay." Telsky stood straight up, but kept his one hand on his chest. "Let's go, but can we walk? I'm thinking my heart's a little charged."

The two crossed the street and headed around the corner to the student parking lot, which had emptied out considerably in the hour they were gone. The only cars left were those that belong to underclassmen. Normally, Nick would have expected Telsky to pull some kind of prank on them but it didn't look like Telsky was able to even remember his own name right then.

When they finally reached Nick's car, Telsky poured himself into the front seat and immediately closed his eyes. Nick was partly pleased that he didn't have to maintain a conversation, and partly worried that the guy was going to croak on him. He drove quickly and quietly across town to Andy's auto parts store. He found a parking spot on the side lot up against the store. When he shifted the car into park, the jolt aroused Telsky enough that waking him would not fall upon Nick's shoulders.

"We here already?" Telsky shifted himself up into a sitting position. "Thank G-d." He pulled at the door handle and jumped out. He spun around and slammed the door shut. Without a word, he was gone... behind the car, toward the sidewalk and around to the storefront, all before Nick was able to get the convertible top up or his seatbelt off. *Not even a thank you. Prick.*

By the time Nick had gotten finished putting his car 'to bed' and entered the store, Andy and Telsky had disappeared into the backroom. There weren't any customers in the store and the cute little girl Andy had hired to be the cashier was sitting on the stool behind the counter filing her fingernails.

"Oh hi, Nick." She barely looked up. She had only met him on Monday, but she was already creeped out by Nick. She had a healthy respect for his seniority at the store, his familiarity with the inventory and his knowledge about cars, but she still thought he was weird. She barely ever said anything to him other than "Hello, Nick."

"Hello Abby. They go in the back?"

Abby nodded.

Nick dropped his backpack in the corner behind the register. There wasn't much he could do if he couldn't go in the back. "So, are you working here full time over the summer or do you have other plans?"

"I'm going away for the summer, but not until the middle of June. You?"

"I graduate next week, so this will be full time until I start college in the fall. Andy said I could continue since I'm going to school locally."

"Cool."

Not a big conversationalist. Maybe if I told you I have no interest in your skinny, pimply ass, you might be a little nicer to me. Or maybe my reputation preceded me. Nobody but my Jeanie will ever turn my head, you little bitch.

Nick decided to straighten stock to pass the time. He started on the back shelves where the windshield wipers were. They were all mixed up and out of order. The makes and models all had to be reorganized. He couldn't figure out how such a simple thing could get so messed up. Before he was able to get too far along, the back door swung open and Telsky bolted out, rushing toward the front door of the store. In a flash, he was gone.

The rest if the afternoon passed quickly. Nick never stopped to look at the clock as he worked feverishly to close the books for May of 1975. His math skills still lacked polish, but were good enough, with the help of a calculator and Andy's old adding machine, to make the numbers work. The purchase orders all matched up and the daily receipts all matched the numbers in his ledgers. *Hmm, seems Andy had himself a pretty good month. He'll be happy to know that. Think his drug business is making him a whole lot more money, though. I wonder how much of that shit he does himself. He always seems so mellow and easy going. Probably not snorting. Probably just dealing. Who cares? As long as he doesn't bring the cops here and keeps me out of trouble.*

Nick packed up his backpack with his personal stuff, including the rest of a sandwich he hadn't finished, figuring he'd probably eat it later in the darkroom. He gathered up the journals and final paperwork to give to Andy on his way out. He poked his head out of the back room to find the store devoid of any customers, or staff for that matter. Andy was sitting at the cash register, leaning back against the shelf behind him, asleep.

"Yoh, Andy man, wake up!" Nick shouted as he stepped out from behind the door. "Time to close up shop for the day."

"Shit, man, already?" Andy roused himself slowly, shaking his head to aid in the process. "Okay, man, well, have a good night."

"Thanks, man." Nick breezed by him, dropping the paperwork on the counter in front of Andy. "I'll be here regular time tomorrow. Back to normal school schedule until the end of next week and then I'm all done." Before Andy could respond, Nick was out the door and on his way to the car.

The ride home was uneventful, as was the ensuing dinner with his family. Nick had resigned himself to the fact that he had nothing in common with any of them, including his brother. Rick had become more and more effeminate as the school year progressed, yet his parents hadn't noticed anything.

Nick wasn't about to out his brother, but had no problem teasing him unmercifully. Rick regularly begged his older brother to not only stop the incessant teasing but also not to say anything to anyone until he was ready to. Rick had no interest in girls, yet he had not experimented with any boys. He only knew he was attracted to them, and that he fantasized about one classmate in particular.

When dinner was over, Rick jumped up, volunteering to clear the table and do the dishes. Surprised by his offer, both Sheila and Norman got up from the table and in unison thanked their younger son. Sheila added, "We're running out to do some errands for an hour or so."

Norman on the other hand, stared down his other son. "Stay out of trouble and don't go anywhere tonight."

"Fine with me." Nick hopped up out of his seat and proceeded to the base of the stairs. "I shall be in my room for the evening then." Nick turned and skipped up the stairs. *Another night in the darkroom with Jeanie. What could be bad?*

* * * * *

The days ran together, becoming monotonous, and Nick's temperament devolved. "Nobody tells you that college is going to be like this. I never have time to study this fucking shit. I have to work so many damn hours to cover tuition, room and board, books, my car insurance and maintenance. And the photography materials are killing me.'

"Wish I could help you, man. I can't give you any more hours than you're already working. Can't afford to pay you time and a half for overtime more than I already am." Andy meant what he said. He was genuinely trying to help Nick.

You could give me some of your drug money to take some weight off. My only other choice is to move back home and I'm not doing that. "I know, man, and I appreciate all you're doing." Nick said as he pulled his Earth Science book out of his backpack. "Do you mind if I catch up on some of my reading when no customers are in the store?"

"Do what ya gotta do." Andy was stoned again, and headed for the back of the store to go sleep it off.

"I got everything covered out here." Nick was actually concerned that Andy was going to let the success of his store slip through his fingers like dry sand. He didn't seem to care much about anything anymore. Every day, for the past two years, has been the same. Andy smokes a joint as soon as he wakes up and continues all through the day. By the time mid-afternoon rolls around, he decides to take a siesta, and sleeps until closing time. Since Telsky got busted and thrown in jail, Andy has been a different person. *He feels guilty. Blames himself. It was him that got Telsky hooked on coke, and Telsky was getting himself into all kinds of skirmishes and doing all kinds of crazy things to get cash to keep up his habit.*

Nick couldn't concentrate on the science text. He had slipped a photo of Jeanie in the book and had forgotten that it was there. He sat behind the cashier counter staring at the picture, and reaching down to rub his crotch, which naturally began to harden at the thought of her. Since she left for college two years ago, he had become more and more obsessive. In those same two years, the only times he's been able to get a glance of her was during winter and spring breaks when she came home to see her father, IF she came home.

This spring, though, Nick was horrified to find a FOR SALE sign posted in front of Jeanie's house. How was he ever going to be able to see her if her family sold the house and moved? *Where are they going to move? Will it be local or out of state? Is she going to come back here or find a job in another city? Is she seeing somebody at college? I should go to her school and see what's going on there? I could probably get some good pictures.*

Nick decided right then that he was going to go up to Georgia and find Jeanie. Emory is a big school, but he was pretty sure he could figure out a way to find her. He didn't have the time to drive up there, but he was confident he could catch a train or even a plane within his budget. *She's so smart. She's at a school like Emory. And I'm down here at a stupid community college. What would she want with me anyway? What if I get there and she has a boyfriend already? I can't let that stop me. I have to have her.*

Closing his science book and rummaging under the counter, Nick found a dog-eared telephone book. The first call he made was to AMTRAK. After fifteen minutes on the phone with them, he had all of the information he needed, finishing the call with the premise that he would call back to buy the ticket when he decided what was the best way to travel. He then called Eastern Airlines. The lady on the other end of the line gave him several different options that not only fit within his budget (which would come directly out of Andy's cash register), but there were several different time options. He made a flight reservation for Friday night with a return flight for Sunday afternoon. All he had to do was figure out a story for his parents.

Chapter 10

Back at the precinct:

"Mrs. Wright, I hate to interrupt you, but I need to know more details about your relationship with the victim. All I have here is that you went to a dance in high school and it didn't end well." Detective Harris got up from his chair and crossed the room to the coffee pot. "Would you like some more?"

"No thank you. I'm pretty jazzed up."

"Okay, so up to very recently, did you see the victim again since high school?"

The detective's interest was piqued. He flipped back through his notes and read for a minute. "You said he used to ride his bike around your house in high school. Would you characterize that as stalking you or maybe just kind of creepy?"

"It was definitely creepy, that's for sure. My friends teased me unmercifully just for being nice to him." Jeanie reached for one of the pens in front of the detective, and instinctively started tapping the cap end on the table.

"So, you didn't answer my first question.

"Well," Jeanie began, "not intentionally. I ran into him unexpectedly while I was in college up in Atlanta." Jeanie stopped talking. She got lost in thought and froze. Posed as if she was a cartoon character, eyes darting back and forth, Jeanie began to piece some things together. "Come to think of it, I don't know how he would have found me there by accident. That's kind of weird. He had some strange explanation, but..."

Detective Harris stood to stretch his legs, beginning a slow pace back and forth behind his side of the table as Jeanie parsed things out. He had the other pen in his one hand, slowly tapping it on the other.

"He only knew that I was going to Emory. I think it was in my second year..." Again, a few minutes of pen tapping, and pacing.

"He hadn't tried to call or write before that?"

"I never gave him any reason to think there was a future for us, certainly not after that dance..."

Detective Harris continued pacing. No questions, no coffee... He finally began to get impatient. "Look you need to give me more than just your suppositions. What do you remember about it?"

"I only know that it was soon after I met the boy, or man who I eventually married. It's kind of weird... the timing of it."

"All right, you're obviously having some difficulty here. Excuse me while I use the men's room and call my wife. I'll be back in about five minutes, and then we'll continue."

"Thank you. May I make my phone call once more?"

"Sure." The detective slipped Jeanie's phone out of his pocket and slid it across the table to her. "I'll be right back."

Jeanie immediately dialed Carl's number, fully knowing this time, that she would get the same result she got the last time, which was only twenty minutes earlier. She then sat wracking her brain trying to make some sense of the events of the evening, and more importantly, trying to find the answers for the detective that would be sufficient for the police to allow her to go home. She knew she had seen Nick at Emory, but didn't remember anything again until recently.

When Detective Harris returned, he was agitated. "Looks like they picked up a suspect." He was short with her. "Well?"

"Really? Already? Who is it? Can I see who it was?" Jeanie was suddenly animated. Then she choked on her words. "It isn't Carl, is it? I mean, I know he was a little pissed at the amount of time I was spending with Nick."

"First of all, no, it isn't Carl. Second, no, you can't see who it is." Detective Harris was beginning to lose his patience. "Can we get back to the questions I have for you?"

"I don't have much more I can say. I do remember that he had his camera with him when he was in Atlanta, and that he took some pictures of me while he was there. Beyond that, I don't remember much.

After college, I don't think I saw him again until a few months ago."

"Let's just keep the dialog going for a little while longer, and maybe you'll remember something else that's key. Why don't you just go freshen up."

Jeanie appreciated the opportunity after drinking two cups of coffee. She left the room and was directed to the women's locker room. The officers told her it would be a lot cleaner than the public rest room.

When she returned, refreshed, she was ready to do some more talking... "That man in the room next door... is he the guy who you think shot Nick?"

"Look, lady, I can't comment on the case other than what we discuss. So, can you please tell me what happened in Atlanta?"

Jeanie slumped down into her chair and got back to what she knew about Nick's trip to Emory University.

CHAPTER 11

"Is anyone sitting there?" Jeanie was startled by the deep voice. She had been sitting in the corner of the small coffee shop in the student union, deeply engrossed in reading her English assignment, and never expected anyone to talk to her.

"Um, uh, no."

"Only reason I ask is that there is not one single chair available in here. You would think they were giving something away. Frankly, I think the food here stinks, but it's the only place to eat between my two classes today, and I only have twenty minutes." The tall fair-haired, well-tanned young man waited for an answer. "Well, do you mind if I sit here?"

"No, not at all. I just won't be very sociable. I have to get a lot of reading done before my next class. I'm not very good with my time management." Jeanie blushed as she realized how handsome she thought the boy was. Her assessment of every one of the opposite sex was still that they were just boys. She still saw herself as just a girl, too.

"Oh, okay, well, my name's Carl. If it's any consolation, I'm not great at managing my time, either." Carl lifted his leg over the back of the one remaining chair and plunked himself down in the seat, allowing his shoulder bag to slide off onto the back of the chair and his tray to land gently on the table. "I won't disturb you anymore after these two questions. One, what are you reading, and two could you pass the salt?"

"Beloved, by Toni Morrison, and yes."

"Hmm, that was easy enough. Read on."

Carl lifted the bread off of the top of his sandwich and lightly dusted it with salt. He gently placed the bun back, twisting it slightly so that it sat exactly the way it was when he disturbed it to season it. Jeanie watched him out of the corner of her eye, noting his propensity for precision.

Jeanie tried to concentrate on her book but found herself watching this young man carefully devour his sandwich, wiping his mouth after each bite. 'Who does that,' she thought to herself. He was certainly persnickety. She laughed inside, imagining taking him back to her dorm room, and watching his horror when he sees what a slob she was.

"Am I distracting you from your work?" Carl had noticed that he was being watched. It didn't make him uncomfortable. In fact, he was intrigued.

"Oh no, I'm sorry. I was actually day dreaming." Jeanie stammered a little as if she had gotten caught with her hand in the cookie jar. "I'm having difficulty concentrating. I let this go a little too long, so I need to focus because I don't perform well under pressure."

"Oh, okay, Well, then don't let me be the reason you don't get your work done." Carl stood up abruptly. He slipped the strap of his bookbag over his arm and then grabbed his tray brusquely. "I need to be on my way, anyway. Perhaps we shall meet again." And he was gone.

Jeanie was stunned. He was gone almost as fast as he had arrived. "Uh... Bye" She tried to look back at her book but found herself watching him leave. She kept her eyes on him only to see him wend his way through the lunchroom to the trashcan, dump his trash and carefully line up his tray with the one underneath, and then sidestep his way through the exit archway until he was out of sight. Jeanie put her book face down on the table next to her tray wondering if she would ever see him again.

There was nothing left to eat on her tray and she had no desire to read anymore. Jeanie glanced at the institutional clock on the wall opposite her table in the corner. If she walked slowly enough, she would only be a few minutes early to her next class. She packed up her things, picked up her bag and tried to emulate Carl as she dumped her trash in the same can, leaving the cafeteria. As she strolled across the campus of Emory University, her mind would continue to take her back to the chance meeting of this guy. He would interrupt her thinking for the rest of the day.

As she walked down Clifton Road toward North Decatur, Jeanie found herself daydreaming. This time, it was not about the book she had been reading. It was about another possible meeting with Carl. He was definitely her type, in looks. Even as she tried to recreate him in her mind, she found herself feeling tingly all over. She hadn't felt that way in a long time. She had dated little since she had been in Atlanta, but there hadn't been anyone special. She had no interest in fraternity life. She had been talked into going to Little Sister Rush by her roommate, who had used the bait of free beer. Jeanie wasn't a fan of beer. She just didn't care for the taste of it. Nobody had prepared her for how raucous those parties could get. She didn't see her roommate for two days after the party. Jeanie had walked home after two hours of being sized up by a bunch of drunken, horny guys. She remembers that feeling of being objectified, reminding her, painfully, of the way she had felt in high school.

Jeanie picked up her pace, feeling suddenly uncomfortable. Someone was walking behind her who had very heavy footsteps. She was afraid to stop and turn around to see who it was. Thankfully, there was a way to see if this person was actually following her or if it was just a coincidence. It could have been that she was edgy because she knew she had not been at her best with regard to school and was suffering from anxiety brought on by her own mismanagement and laziness.

Jeanie ducked into the 1621 building off of Clifton. Whoever it was behind her did not follow. She was able to go out the back door of the first floor through an emergency exit that had the bell disabled, a feature that was well known to the student population. She ambled down a small hill of grass and across a muddy patch to the roadside, leaving her on North Decatur, which was where she needed to be. Glancing again at her watch, she realized that the short cut had deposited her at her destination only five minutes early.

Dropping her bag and her tense body on a bench in the plaza in front of the building, Jeanie decided to read further in her book. She had only a few hours left before her English class and only this class to distract her from her goal.

"Jeanie, is that you?" came a familiar voice from behind her. Nick stood a few feet behind her, trying not to scare her.

"Ooh, Nick, you startled me." Jeanie recognized the voice immediately, but was still surprised to be hearing it. She whipped her head around to find him standing ten feet behind her, against the bushes, wearing the same tee shirt and jeans he wore almost every day in high school. His hair hung limply in the same shaggy greasy style it had always done, only a little longer. The only difference she noticed was an expensive camera hanging around his neck.

"What are you doing up here?" Jeanie asked. "It's good to see you!" Her voice faltered just enough to make Nick question her sincerity. "Are you up here going to school now?"

"No, I'm just visiting a friend over the weekend. Just a guy I know. He's in class right now in this building, I think." Nick kept talking as fast as he could so that Jeanie couldn't cut him off and have a reason to leave. "I met him at Miami-Dade last year and he transferred up here. Smart guy. I didn't know you were in school here." Nick watched Jeanie intently.

"Well, have a seat. It'll be a few minutes before your friend's class is over." Jeanie slid over on the bench and moved her bag to the ground to make room for Nick. "Are you still in school down there?"

"Uh, yeah. I just took a long weekend to come up and check out Atlanta. I was thinking of transferring up here to Georgia State. But I changed my mind." *Now I have to think of a reason why dammit. Why do I say shit like that?*

"Didn't you like the school? Or the city?" Jeanie shifted to the side to face Nick. She was showing real interest in what he was saying.

"Um, not really. That's not really it, though." Nick squirmed, feeling as though he was being interrogated. "I just can't really afford to do it. Can't get the loans and stuff." He paused, again studying Jeanie's reaction. *God, you're beautiful.* "Anyways, I have a part time job at Andy's Auto and I've been doing some photography work... a couple of weddings so far, and I'm trying to save up enough to open a real studio."

"That sounds really exciting for you, Nick. I never knew you were into photography." Jeanie seemed to primp and puff up. "Would you take a picture of me?"

Oh honey, if you only knew. "Sure. Let's look for a good background. You don't want this cement and signs in the picture." Nick stood up quickly and glanced around. "How about over there?" He was pointing over to some hedges on the other side of the plaza.

"I guess so," offered Jeanie. "You're the professional." She slipped her unread book back into bag but as she went to pick it up, Nick grabbed it from her.

"Allow me." Nick yanked the bag out of her hand so hard some of the contents went flying out and landed several feet away.

"Geez, Nick. Some things never change. Relax." Jeanie walked over to pick up her belongings. Frustrated, she returned to Nick and put her books and papers back in the bag.

"I'm sorry, Jeanie. I was just so excited to see you and get to photograph you."

Jeanie's expression shifted noticeably from genuine cheerfulness to one of apprehension. Memories of her 'date' with Nick came flooding back to her, including the aftermath that resulted in a lot of teasing and shaming of both Nick and Jeanie. Nick had gotten very dark and somber during the entire senior year of high school. Jeanie, along with most of the girls, avoided him.

"Let's get this over with so I can go to class." Jeanie's tone had changed and it did not go unnoticed by Nick.

"Don't be mad. I'm sorry."

"I'm not mad. I just have to go."

They walked over to the side of the building. Jeanie did not pose for the picture. She stood, expressionless, in front of a six-foot hedge.

"Come on, Jeanie, at least smile."

"This is the best I can do right now." Jeanie forced the corners of her mouth up.

Nick snapped off several shots. He turned the camera sideways and shot a few more. The clanging sound of the bell that marked the end of class startled him, making the last two or three shots interesting, if nothing else.

Jeanie bolted forward to get her bag. Nick looked down, noticing that her address was in a slot on the inside strap. He hung the camera down, aiming it toward the bag and snapped the shutter one more time, just as Jeanie's hand came into the shot. He didn't know if he was able to get the shot and wouldn't know until the film was developed.

"Was good to see you, Nick. Good luck" Jeanie was already halfway toward the door as she yelled over her shoulder. Nick didn't care. He got what he came for. He had new pictures of Jeanie to fulfill his hunger.

He watched as she disappeared from sight, wondering how he could find out more about her life at college. *Was she dating someone? Fuck that, was she sleeping around with a bunch of these bookworms? Who has her attention? Is it some guy who is going to have is way with her and break her heart? I'll kill 'em. Or is she standoffish like she was with me? Nah, she's a college girl now. She's probably getting laid like all of these tramps who walk around here wearing almost nothing with their tits practically hanging out.*

Nick glimpsed around the plaza. The rush between classes had died down. He rummaged through his back pocket to find the single page map of the campus. It had been sheer luck that he had spotted Jeanie the first time. Now it was time to get real information. He took a quick glance at the map to find the administration building. He was going to see if he could find out where she lived.

It was a long walk across the Emory campus back to the administration building but Nick was more determined than ever to get an idea of what Jeanie was up to in Atlanta. She had become his obsession. His entire life had become centered around her. The new pictures he got of her, with her permission, would go a long way to appease him. The gnawing in his gut, however, had to be quieted. He had to know if she would be available to him when she came home.

While the women behind the desk at the administration office were very nice, they were not very helpful. *Bitch, you need to tell me where she lives. Do I have to make up a story? Do you really want me to lie?*

"I'm her cousin, and I'm only passing through town. I was hoping to just drop in for a quick visit before I head down to Miami to see her Dad. He's not well, you know." Nick tried as hard as he could to sound sincere. He was not very good at sincere. He was getting good at lying, however.

"Well, since you put it that way, I suppose I could tell you the building, and then you could ask the dorm HA for further information." One woman turned her back on Nick and pulled out an old wooden drawer, her wrinkled, less-than nimble fingers walking across the index cards. "Ah, here it is. Your cousin lives on campus at Dobbs Hall."

"Thank you, ma'am." Nick turned on his heels, feeling light-hearted for the first time in a long time. He felt a tinge of hunger, as well. *I'll grab a bite to eat and then go find this place. I'll get me some more pictures and see what she's up to before I have to get back to the airport. This will work out just fine.*

* * * * *

A few hours had passed by the time Nick had found his way through campus to Dobbs Hall. He was feeling satisfied having stopped on campus for a late lunch and a little fact finding about Emory University and the Atlanta area. Content that his Jeanie was in a good place, he walked into the lobby of Dobbs Hall to try to find out Jeanie's room number. He tried asking the girl at the front desk but got exactly the answer he expected.

"Sorry, we can't give out that information."

Bitch. "But I'm her cousin, and I'm just passing through on my way down to Miami."

"Sorry."

"So how do you suggest I find her? I don't even have her phone number."

"I can give you her phone number, but that's all."

"Okay, I'll call her."

With the phone number Nick went over to the lobby phone. He knew she wouldn't be in her room at least until she got back from her class.

"Who you tryin to reach?" A skinny little girl was standing over Nick as he dialed.

"Jeanie Pearlman. She's a sophomore."

"Just passed her in the hallway. She's in 106."

"Oh, thanks." *Sometimes you step in it. I'm never lucky. Thank you, you skinny, little runt.*

Nick stood up and extended his hand to shake, but the girl had turned to leave already. *I wonder if I should even show up at her door. Maybe I better not. She kinda got weird before. Lemme see what things look like outside.*

Before he went outside, Nick did a cursory glance around the lobby, looking for directional or room number signs. He figured out where or about where Jeanie's room would be, and left the lobby, preparing his camera while he walked. He snapped a few pictures of the outside of the building and the grounds.

The Campus police officer didn't seem to think it was fine when he found Nick reaching up his camera, trying to snap pictures through the window of Jeanie's dorm room. He came up behind him and grabbed him by the shoulders, taking out his knees with his, causing him to tumble to the ground.

"What are you up to, son?"

"Uh... nothing sir. I was ... uh... I'm here visiting my cousin... um... she left for class and I forgot to take pictures of her room..." Nick lay breathless on the ground, his face planted in some weeds.

"You sure that's all? I ain't gonna find a neked gurl in that room when I knock on the door em I?"

"No sir, definitely not."

"Well, git along then."

Nick didn't have to be told twice. He scrambled up a slight incline to the sidewalk and skipped into a trot and then found himself running toward the main street to find a cab or a bus. He had his backpack over his shoulder but his camera was still around his neck, bouncing against his chest. *Shit, I can't run trying to hold both of these in place.*

Chapter 12

The years hadn't been kind to Telsky. His reputation and work ethic had followed him long into adulthood, and twenty years later, after time in and out of jail for small drug charges, he was still jumping from job to job and hadn't settled down into any kind of routine. It was Andy who offered some salvation when he hired him to work at the auto parts store.

Andy, too, had been aging. And not gracefully. While he was not in and out of jail, he was still stuck in the seventies, his store doing a modest business and his attitude very much laid back. He was still smoking dope and doing a little dealing out of his back room to supplement his income. His memory was starting to go. His hair was grey, his bones brittle. He thought perhaps he would groom Telsky to take over for him, maybe give him a future.

Nick thought they were both losers. He had at least found a way to earn a living without resorting to crime or drug use. His regular client list was small, but it was an honest living. He did annual family portraits, a few weddings, Bar Mitzvahs, First Communions, and anniversary parties. He had even gotten a few gigs shooting portraits for government concerns. It wasn't a lot but it was enough for him to have a small storefront. He slept on a cot in the backroom, where he had a tiny kitchenette set up in his darkroom. He still had to go to the gym to take a shower, and he didn't do that often, so his appearance remained a little greasy, a little unkempt.

Nick had, however, been following the path of the love of his life to the best of his ability. After she left college, Nick knew she had come back to Miami for a short while, although she wasn't staying with her father. She had been living down by the University of Miami with some guy who was going to law school. Nick had gone down there a few times to spy on her and get some pictures. *The guy was a pencil-necked geek. He was always with the books. Looked like Jeanie was bored to death with this guy. She needed some excitement in her life. She always looked so preoccupied, pensive, almost.*

Soon, Nick lost touch with Jeanie. After a few years, she and her boyfriend had left town and he had no idea where to find her. He had considered reaching out to her dad, but was afraid to. He had no idea what she had told him about what happened that night of the Sadie Hawkins Day Dance. *What if he had an anger problem? What if he held grudges?*

One Monday morning, after a particularly slow weekend, Nick awoke after a fitful night. He fired up a pot of coffee. While it was brewing, he packed up his cot and stowed it under a shelf, loosely draping a curtain over it. He never let anyone in the back of his store. He used the rear of the storefront for studio shots. He didn't want anyone knowing that he lived there.

Nick walked out to the front to see if there was any mail. The postman never delivered it in the box. He was compelled to shove it through the old mail slot in the front door, and it always sat precariously on the welcome mat. It was usually mostly junk mail and catalogues. Occasionally he would find a check in payment of services rendered. That was always a pleasant surprise. He was never good about chasing down open invoices. He hated asking for money.

There was one unfamiliar envelope on this particular morning. He turned around and tossed all but that envelope on the store counter. He recognized the logo in the upper left-hand corner. It was his High School. He ripped open the envelope and slid out the card. It was a Hold-the-Date card for his twentieth High School Reunion.

"Ha! Like I really want to see those losers." He stopped suddenly. *No wonder my dad always told me I was smart but slow on the uptake. Jeanie might come to this.* He slipped the card back in the envelope, the motor in his mind revving up. *I wonder where she is these days, or if she would even come to something like this.*

Nick moved about the store slowly, mindlessly going through the motions of his daily routine of opening up his modest business. He opened the blinds in the small display window, and then turned to the front door, flipping the neon-colored sign from closed to open. He stopped for a moment, glanced at his watch, and then flipped the sign back to closed.

"Nobody is looking for me this early on a Monday morning." There was nobody there to whom he was talking. Nick was quite comfortable being alone. He spoke aloud to himself all of the time. He preferred that to the hum of his old television or the crackle of an old radio the previous lessee had left behind. Nick made his way back to the customer rest room, which doubled as his personal bathroom and his kitchen. During business hours, he removed the toaster oven and the coffee pot. He used the toilet, washed his hands and grabbed a mug from the shelf over the sink. As he poured a cup of coffee, his thoughts returned to the reunion.

Back in the studio room, Nick tried to get comfortable on the one folding chair with his coffee and his imagination. *If she did show up, maybe she would let me dance with her. I could touch her again... Whisper in her ear...*

Before he knew it, the coffee cup was on the floor next to the chair, his sweatpants were down around his knees and he was going at it as fast and hard as he could, screaming Jeanie's name and writhing in the chair. He thrust his pelvis up as his cum exploded forward, shooting out across the floor in front of him. Nick collapsed back into the chair, bare-bottomed on the cold metal, breathless.

Nick slowly opened his eyes. "And that's how it would go." He slowly stood up and pulled up the elastic band of his sweatpants. His coffee had narrowly escaped the barrage from his explosive orgasm, but it had gotten cold over time. He bent over to pick it up and felt a twinge in his back. "Ahh, I must be getting old."

After refreshing his cup, Nick went back to the Studio room and threw on some clean clothes, and then wiped up the floor. He walked unsteadily through the store to open up. It was past 10:00 and he had already been warned by the landlord that he had to be open from 10:00 – 6:00 at a minimum to keep his lease. *Asshole. The photography business is different than a damn candy store or clothing shop. I work nights and I'm a one man show. I have to close early to be at events, and that geek still doesn't get it.*

The newspaper seemed to be getting smaller and smaller as the years went by, and it had nothing of real interest to Nick. Still, he turned to the obituaries first. Ever since his brother passed away, he had been reading the obits first, looking to see who else he knew who had beaten him to the afterlife.

Rick had fulfilled Nick's prophecy, living an openly gay lifestyle, and succumbing to the AIDS epidemic in the mid 1980's.

Rick's death had destroyed his family, although it was his coming out that took his father aback. Norman Lefton never accepted Rick's homosexuality, and the fighting over it led him to leave the family in an angry divorce. He didn't even come to the funeral when Rick finally passed, leaving Nick to take care of his mother.

Mom never got over any of that shit. That's probably what sent her to an early grave. Died of a broken heart. Oh shit... Wasn't that lady in her bridge group.

He looked closer at the newspaper only to find that the name he was looking at was spelled differently than his mother's friend. Just as he turned the page, he heard a rapping on the window of the front door of his store.

Nick poked his head around the door jamb of his back room. He saw a small woman with her face pressed up against the glass, peering in the store. *Guess it's time to go to work.* He took a quick peek at himself in the mirror that hung on the back of the door and then strode through the store to the front door. When the woman saw him coming, she quickly pulled away from the window-glass of the door and hurried away.

Shit. She probably wasn't going to even buy a fucking frame anyway. Nick turned back, and dropping his shoulders looked dejectedly around what he considered to be his greatest accomplishment. He felt suddenly very alone. He was approaching forty years old; he had no immediate family left, save his father who hadn't been in touch in twenty years; the one person he truly loved was with someone else, and had been so since college. He owned no property, as he only paid rent for the storefront. He was living like a hermit in the back of the store. He didn't take care of himself very well, and the only friend he had left was Telsky, and he was no prize.

Nick sighed deeply and leaned on the front counter, thumbing through his appointment book, noting that he did, at least, have a few appointments during the week. A ladies' auxiliary luncheon on Wednesday at a restaurant on the other side of town, a Bar Mitzvah rehearsal on Thursday and then the party Saturday night at a hotel on the Boulevard.

That's a big week. Maybe I can put some money away finally.

After flipping the book shut, Nick went back to the coffee pot to refresh his cup. He then walked back to the front of the store, switched the sign in the door to 'Open' and unlocked both the dead bolts. He then pulled out his ledger to see if there was anything outstanding about which he could make collection calls before he started sending out vendor checks. He was deep in the red this week. He slammed the book shut. *Shit! I can't seem to get out of this hole.*

One more time, Nick picked up and glanced over the reunion invitation. He was determined to go to this thing on the off chance that he could reconnect with Jeanie. He had six weeks to get his act together. He needed to clean himself up, get some nice new clothes; get his car fixed, washed and detailed; and maybe get some fancy business cards printed. *I have to impress her. Let her see how successful I am.*

Nick made one more trip to the back room and pulled the key to his safe out from under the chair cushion. In the back corner of the room, under an old file box, was a metal box-safe. He struggled to slide it out from under the weight of the file box, which was degrading from time and moisture. He finally, having lost all patience, yanked the box out. The thrust of his tug landed him on his bottom and file box on its side, broken at the seams.

Jamming the key in the lock, he flipped the lid open. There, sitting innocently on the top of the contents, was a dogeared photo of a young woman. Her naked back to a window revealed only a slight curve of her supple breast from under her partially raised arm. The picture was slightly crooked and a bit out of focus. Nick stared at the picture for a minute, and finally picked it up. He held it to his chest and closed his eyes. *If only I had more time that day. If only I hadn't gotten caught by that campus doofus...*

Chapter 13

It didn't look to Nick like anyone had changed that much in twenty years. Nobody had grey hair yet. Either that or they were spending a fortune on hair dye. There were a few guys who were balding. The girls all looked the same, that is, the ones who weren't pregnant or just fatter. He recognized a lot of them, even the ones who used to rough him up with Telsky. Then there were Annette's bitches. But so far, no Jeanie. He stood by the registration desk nervously, holding a drink in one hand, and using the other to wipe back his greasy hair every few minutes.

"Are you waiting for somebody specific? Maybe I can see if they're already here or if they are even registered." Nick didn't know the woman behind the desk. The staff of the event was apparently the class behind them and hotel personnel. He shook his head to the negative.

"I'll wait. I want to watch her come in." Nick had absolutely no idea if she was even coming. He had lost touch so long ago. She lived in his mind as a nineteen-year-old college student, the image he carried was the last picture he took of her or the last time he saw her. He never let in that she might look different, or that she might be coming with a husband or boyfriend. In Nick's mind, she was as excited to see him as he, she.

Tilting his glass back, Nick sucked the last of the vodka off of the ice cubes. He glanced at his watch, realizing that it was still before the start time for the event. He walked quickly back to the bar inside the ballroom and got in line. He had used his free drink ticket, so now he would have to dig into his own cash. While standing in line he glanced around the room. He saw nobody with whom he wanted to socialize. He wasn't friends with them in High School and he couldn't see having anything in common with them now.

Glimpsing down at the floor, Nick noticed something shiny. He reached down to pick it up. It was a money clip, stuffed with bills. Slipped in one end, Nick found two drink tickets. He slipped out the drink tickets and put them in his pocket. He then spoke up, "Did anyone drop their cash?" A few of the men in front checked their pockets. Nick added, "describe how you carry it and approximately how much you had..."

"I think it's mine. It should be a small silver money clip with an image of mountains and clouds etched into it... I think I had about two hundred in it." The guy was two or three ahead in line. "Oh, and my drink tickets."

Nick grunted. "Sounds right, but I don't see any drink tickets. Here ya go buddy." *Why do I always clear my throat right before I lie?*

"That's okay, thanks man. Can I buy you a drink? That was nice of you. You could have pocketed it."

"Not to worry. I'm not that much of a drinker and I have my ticket here." Nick had dropped his other hand down behind his back to hide his glass.

"Well, at least trade places in line with me. It'll save you a couple of minutes."

"Thanks, man." Nick moved up, at the same time moving his glass around to the front. *That'll save a minute or two. I wanna get out to the lobby so I don't miss Jeanie.* Nick reached in front of the man in front of him and slipped his empty glass onto a bus tray that teetered precariously next to the bar set up. There were already a few glasses there so Nick's addition would go unnoticed.

"Yeah, hi. Can I get two vodka rocks?" Nick slapped the two drink tickets on the table. "My wife is in the lobby waiting for her best friend. She sent me in to get her a drink, so..." Nick looked around nervously. So far, nobody, not one person had recognized him. He wasn't surprised. Other than being a punching bag for Telsky and his gang and the object of ridicule for a few of the popular girls, he never felt like anyone had even noticed him in high school. He was planning on just laying low. *If she doesn't show up, I'll just have a bite to eat and maybe, if I can scare up some drink tickets, a couple more drinks.*

Nick turned on his heels and hurried back to the lobby. It had, in the time he was gone, filled with a bunch of people of all shapes and sizes. Now he was noticing some beer bellies and some gray hair, a lot of diamonds and gold and a few face lifts, already. He couldn't help wonder why, at only forty, these women were so vain. And there she was. *God, she's as beautiful as she ever was. Is she... isn't there anyone...? She's by herself!* Nick downed one of the vodkas in one and a half swallows, and then bent over, placing the glass on the floor behind the registration table boxes. When he stood back up, he scanned the room to find her again, and saw that she was walking directly toward the table. He quickly ran his fingers through his hair and then patted it back down. *This is it.*

"Nick, is that you?" Jeanie spotted him immediately. As she approached the table, she placed her clutch on the edge, and leaned in to tell the woman her name. Nick didn't hear what she had said as a last name. He was straining to hear if the registration lady would repeat it or ask her a question, but she simply handed Jeanie a name badge. *Shit, why are they only using unmarried names. They could use both. Damn it. Now I'm gonna have to ask her if she's married and that's gonna be awkward. Maybe she'll just volunteer the information.*

Jeanie stepped away from the table with her clutch under her arm as she attempted to peel off the backing from the name sticker. "I'm not the best at multi-tasking. Can you give me a hand?" She stepped over to Nick. "It's really good to see you, Nick. How have you been?"

Nick was, to his surprise, tongue-tied. He reached out and took the badge from Jeanie and mumbled, almost under his breath, "I'm well, thank you, and you?" He methodically peeled off the backing, but did not hazard to reach over to place it on her chest.

Jeanie took the badge from Nick's outstretched fingers, noting that he was shaking. "That's okay, I got this." She slapped it on over her left breast as Nick stared in disbelief. There he was, standing right in front of her, with a normal reason to look directly at her chest, if only for a few moments. Jeanie caught him looking and somehow didn't say anything. She turned her attention to the door as if looking for something or someone.

Nick somehow found the courage to speak out. "Can I get you a drink?"

"Oh no, no thanks. Carl is parking the car. I think I should wait for him."

"Carl?" Nick could feel his stomach drop. He suddenly had the strong sensation of needing to use the bathroom. "Is that your boyfriend? Husband?"

"My husband." She turned back to see Nick staring at his shoes. "We met at Emory. And he came down here to go to law school at UM." She stopped her chatter waiting for some kind of response. Nick still hung his head. "Are you okay?"

"Yeah, I guess."

"Anyway, he's now a junior partner in a small downtown firm, working his ass off trying to make partner. He really didn't want to come tonight. He's probably out in the parking lot smoking a cigar."

Nick saw an opening. "Well, if he doesn't want to be here, what's the harm in going in and having a drink with all your old high school friends. Think I saw a few of your crowd."

"What do you mean, my crowd?" Indignant, Jeanie put one hand on her hip and thrust her clutch in Nick's chest. "You know I wasn't like them."

Nick realized that was true as soon as she said it. Otherwise, she would never be standing there talking to him. "You know what? You're absolutely right. I'm sorry." He paused, cocked his head to the side, attempting to be that sheepish young man in high school. "So, about that drink?"

"Oh okay, what could it hurt. He'll find me."

Nick lifted his arm and offered it to Jeanie, like he had seen done in the movies. It's not like he had anyone to really teach him how to behave with women after his father skipped out. Jeanie responded appropriately, so he figured he was doing well. Arm in arm, they entered the ballroom. Nick thought he heard a gasp or a cough. But he held his head up high. It was as if he had traveled back in time twenty years to high school and had achieved, once again, the pinnacle of all his longing.

"Jeanie... Jeanie Pearlman!"

"Oh darn, I was so hoping she wouldn't be here for this." Jeanie turned her attention directly to Nick. She was making a supreme attempt to engage him in conversation as if she hadn't heard someone calling her name.

"Hoping who wouldn't be here?"

"Annette. Act like you didn't notice her calling my name. Act like I'm telling you the most interesting story and that you're hanging on every word."

"Oh. My. God." Annette put her hand on Jeanie's shoulder and spun her around. "I can't believe you ended up with this guy. Even after..." Annette stopped herself from going any further.

"Annette, stop. First of all, Nick is a nice guy, so just stop. Second, my husband is parking the car, and Nick was nice enough to greet me and buy me a drink, so just stop."

"Stop what? I didn't do anything?" Nick could tell the wheels were spinning as Annette thought about what she would say next. He was prepared to defend the honor of his Jeanie if she said anything bitchy, which is how he remembered her from High School. "I was just surprised to see the two of you together, that's all." Annette looked exactly as she did on graduation day. Thin, pretty and strutting around with an air of false confidence. "So, Nick, is it? Are you still local? What do you do? Are you married? Got kids? Fill me in, Nicky boy."

"Annette, let up." Jeanie, while coming to Nick's defense, was interrupted.

"I got this. You know, Annette, there are nicer ways to talk to people." Nick took a deep breath. "Apparently you haven't outgrown your teen years. But, for the record, no, I'm not married, but I am local.

I have a professional photography business. I do weddings, religious events, corporate events, private portraits and a lot of government work. Does that answer all of your questions?"

'Uh, yes." Annette was humiliated, or at least humbled enough to know not to go down that road with Nick again.

"So, this is what happens when I leave you alone for ten minutes? You find another man to buy you drinks?" Carl came up behind Jeanie and put his arms around her waist, and then kissed her on the cheek.

"Your timing is impeccable. Carl, this is my friend Nick, and this is Annette, someone I knew back in High School."

Nick could feel his heart skip a beat. He was thrilled to be considered in that light. He reached out to shake hands with Carl. Annette, on the other hand, grunted, nodded at Carl and left.

Nick spoke first. "Why don't you find a table. I'll get drinks. What'll ya have, Carl?"

"Well here, I got these drink tickets they sent. I'll have scotch on the rocks, thanks." Carl turned, and putting his arm over both shoulders of his wife, guided her out of the drink line and out into the ballroom. Nick stood motionless, watching their every move, with his back to the bar.

"Hey buddy, you're up." Nick was startled out of his stupor by the bartender. "I ain't got all night. Look at the line behind you."

Although his heart had sunk down into his gut, Nick put two drink tickets and a five-dollar bill on the counter. "I need two vodka rocks and a scotch rocks." He rested his chin in his hands with elbows on the counter while he waited. *She seems happy. I guess that's what I wanted for her. But I wanted her to be happy with ME Dammit.*

Nick half-heartedly picked up the three drinks and slowly walked out into the ballroom. He surveyed the room looking for the couple he would spend an uncomfortable evening with... or would he? *Why am I even doing this? I'm gonna just down this one and get the hell out of here.*

He soon spotted them at a corner table in the front of the room by the corner of the dance floor. He walked slowly across the room trying hard to lose himself in and among the cliques of people chattering and laughing. *Not that anyone would remember me much less say hello...* When he got to the table, he plunked the drinks down on the edge of the table, and then swung his lanky frame around into the only empty chair at the table of six. He quickly looked around at the faces of the other three people sitting there and was relieved to see that they were all strangers to him. It appeared to him, also, that they were not acquainted with Jeanie either.

"What took you so long?" joked Carl. He reached forward and plucked his scotch from the triad of glasses. "I'm just kidding with you, pal. So how do you know my wife?"

"Uh. Um, we had a few classes together back in high school. That's really all."

"You can tell him the truth. Carl," began Jeanie, "we went to a dance together. It was one of those dances where the girls ask the boys out." She stopped, puzzled. "What did they call it?"

"It was, um... it doesn't matter." Nick offered.

"No really, I can't remember. It had a name." Jeanie was visibly distracted by the fact that she couldn't recall the name of the dance.

"It was a Sadie Hawkins' Day Dance, although I don't really know what the genesis of the name is. It was probably some old quaint thing our grandparents did." Nick took a long sip from his third drink of the evening. He was definitely starting to feel the effects of the vodka. "I don't know how I got so lucky that the beautiful and talented Jeanie Pearlman invited me to be her escort for the dance.

"Oh stop. You do yourself a great disservice. You were my knight in shining armor who swept me away from those snarky, snobby girls." Jeanie threw her head back and laughed out loud. She picked up her drink and toasted her old friend. "Here's to heroes and fairytales."

Carl joined in. "To heroes and fairytales."

"Ditto." Nick's heart wasn't in it. He knew that was only a memory and the present didn't offer him much hope. He downed the remainder of his vodka and firmly placed the glass back on the table. "Listen, it was great to see you again, but I have a job early tomorrow. I gotta hit the road."

"But we really didn't even get a chance to talk. Just a few more minutes." Jeanie implored Nick to stay.

"Okay, a few." Nick sat back in his chair. "So, what are you up to? Where to you people hang your hats?"

"We actually live just north of the old neighborhood in a new gated community. It's just being built and they're not even sure what the name of the development is going to be." Jeanie took a sip of her drink.

"Yeah, they were all set to call it Highland Village, but found out there was already a retirement complex by that name." Carl continued. "Since I'm into contract law, I opened my mouth about the name when we signed our building contract. About a month after we signed and they started construction, we got a notice about it. That was a year ago. We've been in the house three months already and they still haven't come up with a name that the current owners can agree on. I can tell that this is going to be some fun Homeowners Association."

"Where do you live. Nick?" Carl asked.

Nick was worried his question would be reciprocated. "Uh, I live over on the boulevard, down around 125th Street." *That's not a lie. It's just kind of stretching the truth. So, what if I don't have an apartment or a house. I just live there, that's all.*

"Oh, okay. I think I know where that is. And what do you do to pay your bills, so to speak?"

"I'm a photographer," Nick said tersely.

"Have I seen your work? I mean, are you a photojournalist? Or What?" Carl seemed to show a real interest.

"Nah, I do more like portraits and events and stuff. Occasionally I get one of my shots into the society page and shit. Ooh, sorry. I mean and stuff." Nick suddenly became extremely self-conscious. He wasn't quite sure why it was important to him to impress this guy.

"Don't have to hold back with me. I've heard all of the seven dirty words you can't say on television. Big fan of Carlin." Carl threw his head back laughing and then took a big swig of his scotch.

"Okay, then, so what do you do, as you say, to pay your bills." Nick felt like he was on the defensive for some reason.

"I'm an attorney. I do mostly corporate law, but I do a bunch of pro bono stuff in just about anything if the spirit moves me enough." Nick's stomach clenched. "I just worked with a young girl who had to fight her brother for a fair shake in an estate settlement. He was trying to rip her off."

"That was nice of you." Nick tilted his glass back and began chewing on the small amount of ice that remained in his glass. "Listen, I really gotta get out of here. It was nice meeting you." *Not really. I was hoping you didn't even exist.* Nick pushed is chair back with his legs and stood up. "Perhaps our paths will cross again."

Carl stood and extended his hand to shake, but Nick had already turned to leave. Carl and Jeanie both called out in unison, "Goodbye, Nick." They looked directly at each other and then, again in unison, whispered, "He's weird."

Chapter 14

Nick woke up with a start when he saw the digital clock on the table beside him. Thinking it was Monday, he jumped up out of the chair and slipped into the bathroom. He lifted the toilet lid and while he was relieving himself, he noticed the calendar hanging on the wall in front of him. "Shit! Its only Sunday. What was I thinking?"

There has to be more to life than this, thought Nick. Last night had been the seventeenth year in a row he had been hired to photograph the Homecoming dance for his old high school. The kids didn't look much different than his fellow students thirty-nine years ago. The only thing that had really changed were the hair styles and the music. It had been a bore and it paid little to nothing. The kids really hadn't changed a bit. Jocks were jocks, bitchy girls were still the same. He was glad he was nearly forty years out of high school.

When he finished in the bathroom, he went over to the front door, still in his jeans from the night before, and opened it. *Good, nobody stole my Sunday paper.* He bent over to pick up the paper, and while doing so, he glanced up and down the hall of the seedy apartment building. *Geez this place is dingy. Someday, I'll get the hell out of here and into a decent place.*

Tossing the paper on the coffee table, the one he got from the thrift shop, Nick sluffed over to the kitchenette and put up a pot of coffee. The one thing he didn't skimp on was his coffee. He had spent a pretty penny on his coffee set up, having spent hours researching it on the internet and finally buying it at the Macy's Cellar. He grinds his own beans every couple of days and brews only two cups at a time, even though he drinks five or six cups a day, now.

When then the coffee was ready, he poured a cup and went back over to his chair, picked up the Sunday Herald and began his ritual Sunday morning. First, he checked the obituaries. It reminded him of his grandfather and that made him smile. *Poppop used to do this. If he didn't see his name, he would say I guess I'll have to shit, shower and shave and then go to work.* Then Nick would read the local section. He didn't bother with the sports section like most men. He just really didn't care. Then he would read the front section and see what was happening in the world.

But this Sunday morning, something caught his eye in the local section. It was a notice on the back page that said, "Calling all Chargers from the Class of 1975," That was him. That was his class. He looked closer. The reunion committee was back at it, this time for the 40th reunion. He squinted to look at the fine print at the bottom to see who was on the committee, and there it was. "Jeanie Pearlman Wright." He stood up and began pacing as he read the remainder of the ad, sometimes to himself, and some of it aloud. "That's next spring." *And it's for a whole weekend at some swanky hotel.* "And she'll definitely be there because she's on the planning committee." *But, so will that husband of hers.*

Nick could hardly contain himself. His heart was pounding and it felt like he had butterflies in his stomach. He felt young again, like he did when he first saw her at school, or when he was daydreaming about her as a kid. He was pacing around the apartment like an expectant father in a hospital waiting room. The only thing missing was the box of cigars. He had the newspaper in one hand and his coffee in the other and his mind was racing.

Sitting back down in his arm chair, he carefully put his coffee cup down and opened the paper back up to the ad. *What do I need to do to be sure I get an invitation? Hmm. Oh, okay. Just call the number or email them with my mailing address.* Nick reached over to the coffee table and rooted through a big glass bowl full of junk, looking for a pen and a scrap of paper. He quickly jotted the phone number from the ad down. *Maybe this is Jeanie's number. Or not. It doesn't matter.*

Nick decided to occupy his mind with other things lest he go crazy waiting for a decent hour to call the number. It was still relatively early on a Sunday morning and if nothing else, he did remember some semblance of manners his mother had instilled in him. He would wait until the afternoon to call. He figured he would go with his original plan and get his laundry done.

Chapter 15

"You know I didn't mean that the way it sounded." Carl stood at the foot of the stairs. "Jeanie, come down and let's talk this out before I leave for the office."

"No." Jeanie stood in front of the mirror in the upstairs bathroom, wiping the tears away. Carl has been doing this more and more, and she was never good at being yelled at. She didn't grow up in house with yelling and she still, after thirty years, can't get used to it. "We'll talk when you get home. Besides, I don't have time now."

Carl left abruptly, allowing the door to slam behind him. He stomped down the few stairs and out to his car, slamming that door as well. He and Jeanie had been fighting a lot lately, and he wasn't sure why. He was aware that she was going through the change, whatever that meant, but he never knew what to expect. He didn't think he was doing anything that bad. He hadn't really changed much other than the boat. She seemed excited when he bought it.

Jeanie finished putting on her make-up and then tripped down the stairs, taking two at a time. She didn't stop for a cup of coffee, but when she reached the front door, she stopped. Pulling the curtains to the side, she watched as Carl pulled away before she opened the front door to leave. She wanted to avoid another confrontation. As she closed the door behind her, her cell phone rang, but buried deep inside her purse, she didn't attempt to answer it. It was likely another reunion inquiry, so it could wait until she got to the meeting.

Driving up I-95 during rush hour was not pleasant for anyone, least of all, Jeanie Wright. Every time she turned on to the entry ramp, she would flash back to the night she and Carl had to rescue her daughter after the accident. She would relive every single moment of a harrowing experience, every week of sitting by her side in the hospital, every month of taking her to physical therapy and every hour in the courtroom until that bastard got sent to jail for drunk driving. And, every tear shed for Julie, her daughter's friend, who died in the crash. It was ten years ago but the memory haunted her.

Jeanie merged into the traffic slowly, because she had no choice. It was bumper to bumper all the way up to Fort Lauderdale, and didn't let up until she was finally headed westbound on 395.

Jeanie finally relaxed her shoulders enough to turn on the radio. Thankfully she was finally getting satellite radio and didn't have to listen to news or advertising. She tuned in to a soft rock station and lost herself in some music from James Taylor, the Eagles and Carole King. This was music from her teenage years and made her feel safe and comfortable.

When she reached the hotel, she parked far enough away so that there were no cars on either side of her. She didn't have confidence in her parking ability, even still, since her driver's education days. She can still hear the drivers' ed coach screaming at her when she nicked the car by hitting the traffic cone. She barely hit it and it was as if she had committed mortal sin.

She wasn't even sure why she decided to serve on the committee for this thing. Her thoughts were swirling around in her head as she walked through the parking lot and toward the main entrance of the hotel. Meeting these women to plan the weekend was not necessarily something she was anticipating with any great joy. She wasn't friends with nor remembered any of them. The only reason she was there was because she lived locally. So many people moved away after high school and college.

The women met up in the lobby with the hotel's event planner. After a quick tour of the facilities they would be using for the reunion, they were treated to lunch in the coffee shop where they talked room number guarantees and rates, menus, and access to the business center, gym, spa and honor bar charges. Jeanie, who had started the day in a bad mood, was impressed with the hotel and what it had to offer. She was even warming up to the theme upon which the other three women had already decided. While she more like a third wheel, and wasn't really contributing much to the conversation, she felt relieved to have something to keep her mind occupied and not obsessing on Carl and his boat.

"What do you think, Jeanie?" One of the women asked her opinion, although her mind had drifted off.

She was focused on the lobby and the crystal chandelier, wondering how something like that would look in her foyer.

"I'm sorry? I was distracted." Jeanie was openly embarrassed. "What was the question?" Suddenly Jeanie reverted back to her high school self. She was unprepared, self-conscious, and shy.

"We were discussing table covers. Whether we wanted to do a solid color, say red, or have a white lace overlay on top." Jeanie looked blindly at her as if she was speaking a different language.

"Either is fine. I thought we weren't doing an overload of decoration. So maybe the overlay would be a nice touch." She knew she was talking in circles, but then that's what these women did all the time when they were making these kinds of small decisions.

"Good thinking." The caterer jotted that down on her paperwork. "I think that takes care of everything we need to do today. If you'll just get me a deposit three months before along with the room block, and I'll start to need numbers about two weeks in advance for the kitchen.

"Sounds good," said one of the ladies. Jeanie didn't have any idea who was who anymore. Then the lady turned to her. "Jeanie, I'll be back in town in about three weeks and we can meet again then, okay?"

"That would be good." Jeanie stood up. "And I've gotten a lot of feedback from the ad I placed looking for alumni. I'll send you an update on my list when I get home."

"Perfect."

The three women left the hotel coffee shop together, but in silence. They all were lost in their own thoughts. Two were concerned about making flights, the other about facing another fight.

* * * * *

Jeanie walked slowly through the parking lot with her folder under one arm and her purse slung over her other shoulder. Her mind was racing, thinking about all she had to do yet this day. She had to stop at the dry cleaners for Carl's shirts, the pharmacy for his prescription and the grocery store for something for dinner. She had to clean up that list and forward to the committee. She wanted to get a load of laundry done before dinner because there was a documentary on television she wanted to watch. She looked up and didn't see her car.

A slight panic came over her. There was a small bead of perspiration forming over her brow and over her lip. She spun around on her heels, only to spot the car directly behind her. Jeanie was not normally the type of person to become alarmed over things like this. Not anymore. It was happening more often, though, because she had been fighting more with Carl. That was her justification for it, anyway.

The parking lot was marked in a very specific way and Jeanie just wasn't having it. Her car was parked at the end of the aisle of a one-way lane, but she pulled out and went the wrong way to get directly out to the exit. It was uneventful, but it somehow made Jeanie act as if she had gotten away with something. She put her blinker on and slipped into the exit lane and pulled out into traffic. The whole way home, while the radio was on, she didn't hear it. She was practicing her fight with Carl. She was lining up her attack lines and her defense lines. Somehow, this seemed to pass the time much quicker than singing along with Carly Simon or Elton John.

Jeanie took the turn into the driveway a bit too fast and hard, scraping her passenger side bumper on the curb. "Shoot. He's gonna kill me." She hit the garage button and slowly pulled in, angling as far to the right as she could, figuring he wouldn't see the damage that way.

Jeanie got out of the car and popped the trunk. Once again, she slung her purse over her shoulder so she could grab all of her packages. She put the pharmacy bag into the grocery bag. She slipped her hand through the holes in the bag and grabbed the shirt hangers. She slammed the trunk shut with her free hand, barely holding on to her keys as she did so, all the while praying that Carl had left the inside door unlocked.

"Of course not, you ass." Jeanie fumbled, one-handed, with her keys to find the right key. "Ah for the good old days when the kids were home after school." She finally made her way into the kitchen, dumping all of her packages, including her purse, onto the kitchen table. She glanced at the phone to see how many messages were waiting, and slovenly trudged up that back stairs with Carl's shirts.

Jeanie came back down to start dinner, although she really didn't feel like doing anything nice for her husband. He had been hell bent on having his way with this boat thing. It offended her that he went out and did it without even telling her. He spent an exorbitant amount of money on it and he's gone every weekend, now. She found herself slamming pots and pans around and ripping open packages of meat and seasoning. "If I did something like that, you'd have my head." She practically threw the roast into the pan. Shaking the seasoning as if it were a tambourine, she found herself close to tears. "This isn't a reason to break up a marriage. Why are you doing shit like this? There has to be a reason you don't want to be here." She slammed the pepper shaker on the counter. "What is going on?"

Jeanie crumpled down into a chair at the table and wept. She would have called a girlfriend but nobody was around. She was one of the few of her circle that wasn't working full time or traveling. She couldn't call either of the kids and she certainly didn't want to upset her mother. This was something she would have to deal with herself.

Glancing at the digital clock on the microwave, Jeanie realized she had to get the roast in the oven or it wouldn't be done in time. She pulled herself up out of the chair and returned to the other side of the island, and then finished seasoning the roast. She turned the dial on her oven, then opened the door, and gently slid in the roasting pan. Under her breath she mumbled, "I don't know why I'm going out of my way. I should just give you hot dogs."

Jeanie cleaned up the counter where she had been working and then pulled some potatoes out of the refrigerator. Angrily, she peeled and cut them. She dropped them in a bowl with some salt water and then cleaned up everything else. The clock blinked 4:18. That would give her some time to take a short nap.

Upstairs, Jeanie kicked off her shoes and stretched out on the loveseat in her bedroom. She clicked on the television, turning the volume to low. She normally detested daytime television so she found some local news, curled up with a coverlet and went to sleep.

CHAPTER 16

If I have to take one more picture of a screaming baby and then listen to the mother say that he's never like this, I think I'll put a gun to my head. Why does every mother think their kid is fucking perfect? Damn rug rats.

Nick bent over to pick up the bigger pieces of cookie and the dirty tissues that were all over the floor of his photo studio room. Tossing them in the trash he begrudgingly grabbed the boom and swatted at the floor, rather than sweep it, firing crumbs and cheerios everywhere. Accomplishing nothing but making the problem worse, he collapsed in an armchair in the corner of the studio. *I gotta get out of this business. I hate kids.*

Silently Nick sat in the chair thinking about ways in which he could move away from doing the holiday photo shoots. *At least its better than the old jobs shooting Santa shots at the mall. That was the worst. This is such a slow time otherwise. No weddings, no family reunions or graduations, no proms. I haven't done Homecomings in years. I guess I'm stuck with the snot nosed kids.*

Nick heard the whine of his front door mail slot squeaking. He bent over and strained his neck to glimpse around the door jamb to see a small pile of envelopes on the floor and the slot still stuffed with some magazine. He forced himself to push out of the armchair and sluffed through the store to the front to pick it all up. He was in no real hurry because he was sure it was a stack of vendor bills and a bunch of junk mail. There was, however, one over-sized envelope in the mix with a shiny surface and a beautiful computer-generated calligraphy font for the address and return address. It was from his old high school. Immediately, he dropped the rest of the mail on the cashier counter at the front of the store and tore into the large envelope. The Class of 1975 cordially invites you...

Nick's heart skipped a beat. He rifled through all the paperwork to find the response card and envelope. Without reading the contents, he quickly marked up the card, putting the number one in every activity category. He planned on attending the Welcome Cocktail party on Friday night, the Poolside

Breakfast on Saturday morning, the Beach Volleyball game on Saturday afternoon, the Main Event on Saturday night and the Sunday brunch on the last day. He reserved a single room and filled out all of his personal information.

When Nick pulled out his wallet to retrieve a credit card, he first realized how much the weekend was going to cost him. He hesitated for a minute, but then scratched out the numbers and expiration date. He stepped back feeling accomplished. *Shit, now where am I going to find a current picture. The old school picture is easy. Got plenty of those in my closet.*

After rifling through various drawers and boxes, Nick found a dog-eared photo that Telsky had taken of him the day he moved into his apartment. He then went back into the closet where he had posted a few pictures of Jeanie, a mini-gallery of her, not unlike the entire room he had dedicated to her at home. He found one of the two of them from the night of the Sadie Hawkins Day Dance.

Nick stuffed the two photos and the response card into the pre-stamped envelope, sealed it, and headed for the door. He opened the door and glanced down the sidewalk in both directions to see if anyone was headed toward his store. The area was barren, giving him plenty of time to get down to the corner and drop the envelope in the mailbox. He turned on his heels and found himself light on his feet, almost skipping, back to the store.

How the hell am I gonna pay for this? I don't spend that kind of money on a two-week vacation. I'm just gonna have to really cut back on shit for the next six months. Nick swung open the door of his store. Suddenly he realized that the return address on the card he just mailed was not the school's address. *Was that going to a committee member? Was it Jeanie?*

Once in the store, Nick shuffled through all the papers that came with the invitation to see if there was any information on the committee. There it was. For questions or more information call Jeanie Pearlman Wright if your local at …. Again, Nick's heart fluttered. He wasn't sure if it was because he hadn't taken his meds or if he was just excited.

The rest of the mail, as he had suspected, was junk or bills, reminding him that he had fallen behind on printing and delivering on some of his orders. He decided to call Jeanie that evening after work and to pass the time, he would try to get some of his backorders filled.

Nick thumbed through his order book to see how far behind he had gotten, sliding out several wedding files. The weddings were his most cumbersome jobs because there were so many photographs, yet they were the most interesting, because he enjoyed doing the touch-up work as well as playing with the filters. The best part was when he finished these, there was no printing to do as the families had to first select the pictures they wanted in the albums and the ones they wanted printed.

After a few hours, he had completed work on four weddings that he had shot in the last month, He fired off the emails with the links to his website and posted a handful of each on his Facebook page.

Next, he pulled out some printing jobs. He noted that he was past deadline on two of them, so he loaded his printer and got the first job going. While that one was printing, he started work on some of the holiday card proofs. *Ugh, these kids. Every damn one of them had to have a fucking temper tantrum. Hello. Mom. The kid doesn't want to do this. Go to the fucking drugstore and buy a box of fucking Christmas cards.*

Nick continued working mindlessly for hours. He boxed up the two print jobs, wrapped them in brown paper and marked the addresses appropriately. They were both local, in fact, so he decided to drop them on his way home. He had been able to complete everything except the three sessions he shot that morning, so he emailed the proofs as well as the available card styles.

He finally stood up to stretch, and noticed that the whole store seemed darker than usual. His initial thought was that a light bulb blew in the main store. He walked out into the store and realized that it had gotten dark. Since he hated wearing watches, and the wall clock's battery had been dead for several weeks, he had to go back to the bathroom to check the coffee pot's digital clock. When he realized it was already after seven, and that not only had he worked through lunch, he was past his usual dinner hour, he quickly shut down all of his equipment.

Nick grabbed the two print orders that had to be delivered, through his backpack over his shoulder and grabbed the balance of the reunion invitation on his way out the door. Thoughts of talking to Jeanie popped back into his head and his gait quickened, almost developing into a skip.

Nick tossed everything into the front seat of his Cutlass, jumped in and revved the engine. Once again, it backfired. *I really need to do something about that. Shit. No, I don't. That's part of what gives it its charm.* He had finally registered it as a Classic Car, and was going to start displaying it at some local car shows. *Who knows where that may lead?*

After making his two drops and a quick run at a drive-through, Nick had finally gotten home. He drove around the parking lot but couldn't find a space. He hated parking on the street in his neighborhood. It wasn't the nicest area. There were a lot of shady characters on the streets, and there have been a few shooting incidents. He needed to protect the only thing of value he had as best he could.

Just about to give in, Nick saw a car at the end of the back row begin to back out. He spun around the opposite end and sped up, turn signal on, and reached the spot just as the other car was pulling away. Nick had a habit of competing for things when he didn't have an opponent. The parking space was clearly his. There was nobody else vying for it, yet he felt compelled to rush in.

Grabbing his dinner, the invitation and his backpack, Nick didn't even wait for the elevator. He skipped up the stairs, taking them two at a time. Once inside his apartment, he dropped his backpack by the door, the bag of food on the kitchen table and the invitation on the kitchen counter. He couldn't decide what to do first. He was hungry, but he really wanted to hear Jeanie's voice. It had been twenty years. I *know if I'm hungry I'll be foggy. I know that. Better I eat first.*

Before he knew it, there was nothing left but a few cold French fries. Nick wiped his hands with a napkin and then picked up his drink. He coughed to clear his throat, and, picking up the invitation, he headed back through his small apartment to his bedroom. Sitting on the edge of the bed, he reached into his pocket and pulled out his flip phone. One of the few things he inherited from his father was his frugality. *The thing still works. When it dies, I'll get a smart phone. For now, this is fine.*

Glancing at the clock, Nick wondered if 8:45 was too late to be calling Jeanie. He knew her kids were long gone. He wasn't sure, though, whether or not she was working or if she was still married. He figured it wasn't yet nine, so it was probably okay.

Nick found the number again in the small print on the invitation. He carefully punched the numbers on his phone and then pushed the little green receiver button. After a second, he heard the call connect and then the familiar ringing sound. And again. And again. And again. Nick was counting the rings in his head. When it reached six, Nick, frustrated, flipped his phone shut.

Maybe she has caller ID. Maybe she knew it was me and she didn't want to talk to me. What if it's that? What if she remembers what happened that night at the dance? She must hate me. She can't hate me. I've seen her since. Stop it, Nick. Maybe she was just on another call. That's it. She couldn't interrupt the other call. Or maybe she left her phone in another room. Yeah, that's it Did I remember my meds this morning. Oh, that's right, I never ate lunch. But there was no voice mail. I couldn't even leave a message. I better go take my pills. Think I'll just take a shower and go to bed.

Nick switched on the television so he had something to take the noise out of his head. He moved toward the bathroom, undressing along the way. Reaching in to turn the water, he faintly heard music coming from the television, a song that took him back forty years. In fact, he recalled, it was the theme song for his class prom, and although he did not attend the event, he remembers the song well. "We may never pass this way again." He sang and hummed in the shower, pleasuring himself while thinking of Jeanie. When he climbed out of the shower, his mind had calmed down, as had his body.

Nick, barely dried off, slipped under the cover and curled up around his pillow in the fetal position. He rocked back and forth for a short while until he fell off to sleep, thinking to himself, *tomorrow is another day, dammit*.

Chapter 17

The interrogation room seemed to take on an unnerving atmosphere. Jeanie put her head down on her arms, burying her face. "I can't take much more of this. I really need to hear from my husband."

"Do you want to try to call one more time? They're likely finished with your phone by now."

"That would be nice, please." Jeanie picked her head up, offering the best smile she could muster. She had been answering questions for over an hour and a half and she was exhausted, worried and still in shock.

Detective Harris jumped up and left the room, leaving the door partly open. Jeanie cocked her head to the side, trying to focus on the man sitting at the far desk facing her. He looked familiar to her, but without her glasses, she couldn't quite tell for sure.

The detective returned, she asked him bluntly, "is that guy out there-- is that Jimmy Telsky?"

Detective Harris was taken aback. "Do you know the guy?"

"Yeah, he went to my high school too. Fact is, I think he was kind of friendly with Nick."

"We have a few questions for him, that's all."

Jeanie sat idle, staring at her coffee cup, taking slow, shallow breaths. After a few minutes, she gave in to the tedious monotony of the silence. "Okay, so you wanted to know the next time I saw Nick. He contacted me because I happened to be on the Reunion Committee and he had a question."

The detective had assumed his position at the table directly opposite Jeanie, looking straight at her. "That's it? There was nothing else?"

"I called Nick. I called him tonight because he had been a support for me when my husband and I were having some issues. That's it. I told you, there was nothing going on."

Jeanie's ire had been raised. The detective was pushing her. "Carl and I are fine now, after a few visits to a marriage counselor and working on those issues. That's kind of why Carl went on this fishing trip."

Jeanie softened. "He earned this getaway weekend with his buddies."

"Earned it?" The detective was curious now and sat up in his chair. He put his glasses back on and picked up his pen. "What exactly do you mean by that?"

Jeanie actually smiled as she gave her answer. "He was not in favor of airing our dirty laundry with a total stranger. So, I kind of had to bribe him to go to counseling. I promised not to give him any aggravation about going on his next 'Man Trip,' as he calls it, the next time one came up." She stopped and looked at the detective. "Are you married?"

"Yes ma'am, I am."

"Does your wife give you a hard time about the time you spend away from her?"

The detective pushed up his sleeve and then glanced at his watch. "As a matter of fact, yes. She's probably wondering where in the hell I am tonight. So, let's get on with this, shall we?"

"Okay, sure. So, Nick and I had met for coffee a few times over those couple of months, that's all. I called him tonight because I knew he'd be around and could kind of help me, waiting to hear from the Keys. There is absolutely nothing romantic going on. But still, I really don't know what happened after he arrived. He opened the car door for me, and I sat down. Next thing I remember is the police showing up. I'm sure I'll remember more as I calm down."

Chapter 18

Nick rolled over and reached for the watch on his night table. He picked it up, and squinting, he realized it was only 6:30 in the morning. His bedroom was dark, but it always was. He had installed black out shades the day he moved in, knowing that he needed total darkness to go to sleep and he didn't have any particular fondness for brightly lit places anyway.

It was Saturday. He didn't have to open the store. He didn't have any appointments or events. He had gotten caught up with most of his printing and shipping work. He put the watch back down on the edge of the table, and rolled back down on his pillow. Staring at the ceiling he contemplated what was ahead for him. *I'll go back to sleep for a few hours, and then get up, get my act together and then call Jeanie at a reasonable hour. I'll just play dumb, like I don't know who I'm calling. Geez, I better think of a good reason to be calling since I already sent in the card.*

Wracking his brain, Nick came up with several scenarios, finding fault with each one. After a few minutes, he sat up in bed. Creativity was not his forte. He began rocking from side to side, while a feeling of anxiety was building inside him. In no time, he found himself scratching at his knees and pulling at his earlobes. *I'm such a fuck up. I can't even come up with a lie.*

Nick threw himself back on the pillow and smacked his arms down at his sides, stiffening his entire body as if trying to force an idea from his lower extremities up through his torso up into his head. Suddenly, he began shaking and twitching, thrusting his chest up and head back. His body contracted and contorted and he began to make guttural sounds, as saliva formed around his mouth. The twitch and jerking continued for a full minute.

As fast as it began, his seizure subsided. Nick remained silent with his eyes closed. He hadn't suffered a full seizure in several years, but then he hadn't been chaotic and careless with his medications, either. Ever since he received the invitation to his reunion, he had been preoccupied with the idea of seeing all those people again, especially Jeanie. His attention to his own personal welfare had gone by the wayside.

Nick had fallen back to sleep for several hours, and when he awoke, he was unaware that he had even had a seizure. He slowly climbed off the bed and stumbled into the kitchen to start a pot of coffee. He then returned to the bathroom, taking care of his morning ablutions. He picked up his razor, deciding at that moment, and for no apparent reason, to start taking better care of himself. He got into the shower afterward, washing his hair and actually repeating the process, like it says on the shampoo bottle. This was something he had gotten out of the habit of doing for two definitive reasons: one, he didn't care how clean his hair was, and two, it saved him money on shampoo.

After his second cup of coffee and a glance through the Miami Herald, Nick turned his focus to his cell phone, sitting on the end table in the living room. He knew it was late enough on a Saturday morning to call, but he hadn't yet come up with any good reason to do so. After pondering the idea for only a few seconds, he decided to cast his fear aside and just make the call.

He would rely on his own ability to make conversation on the fly.

Picking up the phone, he felt a flutter in his chest. When he realized that the phone number was already saved in the phone, he took a deep breath and pushed the redial button, and sat back down at the kitchen table.

"Hello?"

Nick paused. "Um. Hello." He paused, uncomfortably, again. "Is this the correct number to call with questions about the Charger reunion?"

"Yes, yes, it is," came a soft voice from the other end of the line.

"I already sent my response in, but I was wondering if there were a lot of singles coming." Surprisingly, Nick was quite at ease. "Is there a possibility that anyone is setting up shared rooms? I mean, I registered for a single, but it would be really helpful if I could share the cost with another single man."

"Oh, my goodness. I don't think the committee even thought of making that provision. What a wonderful idea!" Jeanie was being sincere. "May I ask to whom I am speaking?"

"Sure, this is Nick Lefton." Nick spoke confidently. "I signed up to participate in every single activity, because I'm really looking forward to the weekend, but I'd love to knock a few hundred bucks off the bill if I could share a room with another guy."

"Nick, it's me, Jeanie!"

"Well, what do you know! How are you, my Jeanie?" As soon as he said it, he was sorry. "What has it been, twenty years?"

"It was the twentieth reunion, wasn't it?"

Nick knew exactly when it was. "I believe you're right! How are you? And your husband? Kurt, no, Carl, is it?" He didn't want to sound too on top of things.

"Wow! That's some memory!" Jeanie sounded genuinely surprised. Nick was pleased.

"So, while I don't want to sound like I'm down on my luck or anything, that's some swanky hotel you're using for the reunion. Its right in the middle of my slow period so my cash flow will be off. Any way there's a room sharing deal?"

"No, but what a great idea." Jeanie stopped talking. In that split-second silence, Nick worried that Jeanie thought he was lame.

Poor, poor Nick. He can't even afford the hotel. I guess he never made anything of himself, That's too bad. "Jeanie, you still there?"

"Oh, I'm sorry. I was just trying to figure this out, now that the invitations are already out." Again, silence.

"Tell you what. How about we talk about it over coffee."

"Sounds terrific. When?"

"It's Sunday morning. It's early. How about around eleven? Wait, where do you live?"

"I live in the Aventura area. Pretty close to the old High School! Where are you?"

"I'm down by Sans Souci," he asserted, even though he knew that was a lie. He lived over on the seamy side of North Miami. "I have no problem coming up your way. I need to get to the mall later anyway. So how about the Starbucks on the Boulevard at around 187th?"

"Perfect. Carl is out on his damn boat, so I have all day. I'll see you at 11:00 then."

Nick stood frozen with the phone in his hand, in total disbelief that he had the nerve to call Jeanie, much less make a date with her. He heard the click. He knew she wasn't still on the other end of the line. Still, he stood with the phone in his hand, imagining how things might go.

I am so happy to see you again after all these years. You look wonderful. Time has been good to you.

'You too, Nick. You haven't aged a day. You are as handsome as I remember.'

Oh, shut up, Nick. She would never say that. She's married. She did sound angry at him, though. Let me try this again.

So, does Carl leave you alone all day often? That sounds really creepy. I can't say that. So, what kind of boat does Carl have? My dad used to have a boat. That's a lie. Shit! What the hell am I going to say to her?

So, Jeanie, what are you doing with yourself these days? I mean, besides party planning? Yeah, that's better. That sounds normal. Then I'll take it from there.

Nick was still standing with the flip phone open in his hand. He looked down at his hand and noticed the time. "Dammit! Why do I always do that?!" He tossed the phone on the couch as he darted into the bedroom closet and frantically looked for something clean and unwrinkled to wear.

* * * * *

Sitting by the window in the corner of the Starbucks gave Nick a good vantage point to see every direction from which Jeanie could possibly enter the store. His knee bounced under the table; his fingers fiddled with the napkin holder. His head snapped back and forth, eyes glaring at each entry. All he could do was berate himself for arriving too early. He could feel the eyes of the Sunday morning regulars staring at him, wondering who he was. Did they think he had a bomb in his backpack? Did he think he was a homeless person waiting for someone to mercifully buy him a cup of coffee? *Did I come my hair? Do I look pathetic? Am I going to scare her off?*

"What are you looking at?" Nick snapped at the young couple sitting at the table next to him. "Haven't you ever seen someone waiting for a person before?"

The young woman turned away, but her male companion started to slide his chair back and stand up. "What if we are looking at you?"

"Honey, stop."

"Yeah, honey, stop." Nick mocked the girl.

The young man sat back down. "You're not worth messing up my serenity on a quiet Sunday morning."

"Mneh, Mneh, mneh, mneh." Nick whined.

He looked toward the front door of the store and there she was. He stood up, pushing his chair back roughly, knocking it over behind him. He barely noticed. He stepped out from behind the table and offered an affectionate wave, motioning Jeanie to join him.

By the time Jeanie reached the table, Nick had not only picked up his chair, but had pulled out the chair for her.

"Ah, and I thought chivalry had died in the last millennium." Jeanie delicately took her seat, sliding the handle of her purse on the back of the chair as she sat.

Nick quietly sat down, not missing the opportunity to sneer at the man next to him. Jeanie hadn't seen the antics that let up to it, nor did she see the final act, so he didn't have to explain anything. "So, can I get you something? Coffee, Cappuccino? Tea? Something to eat?"

"Slow down!" Jeanie took a deep breath. "Okay, first, nothing to eat. But I would like a large American coffee. Nothing special, whatever they have. And I take it black." She wriggled around in the wooden chair, trying to get comfortable. "I hate the chairs here."

"I'll tell you what. I'll go put the order in, and you see if there are any seats over there where the couches are."

Nick stood up and headed over to the counter, while Jeanie stood and glanced around looking for a corner nook or a secluded area in the living room pit. She picked up her purse and moved stealthily toward the corner near the door through which she had entered. There were two occasional chairs with cushions and a small parsons table in the corner. She tossed her purse on the table and a notebook on one of the chairs. She sat down on the other chair, snuggling down into it, reveling in the comfort. "Much better."

Nick returned with a paper tray containing two cups of coffee and some biscotti. "I never ate breakfast. I hope you don't mind." He sat on the edge of the chair and waited for Jeanie to move her purse. He slid the tray carefully onto the table, and then reached behind to retrieve her notepad from under him. "There's plenty of biscotti, so help yourself."

"Thanks, but no. Watching the waist and I already had my breakfast." Jeanie took a quick sip of her coffee. "So, I think you have a really good idea. I just have to figure out a way to implement it now that invitations are already out. I guess I could send a group email and offer that up. I imagine the committee will have to put their two cents in on this." She took another sip, and then gently put her cup on the tray, breaking off a small piece of biscotti before sitting back in her chair. "I have no willpower."

Nick liked the sound of that. Maybe he did have a chance with her. "They are hard to pass up. I love them here."

Nick sat, immobile again. He searched his mind, trying to remember what he had decided to say. Empty. *Dammit. I had it all figured out. What the fuck is wrong with me?*

"So, tell me, Nick. Are you still doing a lot of work with the old school? Or are you getting close to retiring? Last we spoke I think you said you were doing a lot of weddings and some government work?"

"Well, to be honest, I am not planning on retiring any time soon. I like to travel and I'll definitely need to continue working just to finance that. Nothing like National Parks for a photography buff." Nick didn't want to admit that he was living paycheck to paycheck, but that whole story came out of nowhere. "I still do work for a lot of the schools for yearbooks. You know, portraits, team pictures and the like. I've stopped doing a lot of the event work. It's getting to be too much to do all those nights and weekends." He took a sip of his coffee, mainly to give himself time to think. "I guess we're all getting older."

"That's the truth." Jeanie stared off at all of the people in the store. Most of them were younger, engaged in their personal technology. Most of them were wearing earbuds and were not even aware of the people with whom they were sitting. "I think I'm glad I'm where I am in my life."

"Not sure I know what that means."

"Just that we are here, talking with each other, enjoying each other's company."

Now that sounds hopeful. Again, I'm not really sure what you mean, but I'm happy you like being with me. "Still don't... um ...."

"Look at these kids. All with the headphones. Not one of them talking with each other."

"Ahh, now I see." Nick felt a sinking feeling. He thought it was about him. He actually thought she was happy to be with him.

"So how is all of your family? Carl? Your daughters?"

Jeanie half smiled. "Well, both of my girls are now away at college. One is at the University of Florida in Gainesville, and the other went up to my alma mater,

Emory." Nick could see her pride. But he then noticed how she dropped her shoulders, almost sinking back into the chair.

"Are they doing okay? I mean, you don't seem... I mean, um..."

"No, they are doing really well. I'm really proud of both of them. It's that, well, oh ..." Jeanie stopped.

"Hey, if you don't want to talk about it, it's okay. I'm a good listener, but I do get it if its personal."

Jeanie looked straight at Nick. "I've known you almost my whole life. It has been years since we've been together. I feel like it's not right to unload on you."

"That's fine. Just that it might make you feel better."

"Maybe."

"Think about it. Have some more biscotti and coffee."

Jeanie did that. Her eyes glazed over as she stared over Nick's shoulder. They didn't speak for a few minutes. Nick noticed that tears had formed in the corners of Jeanie's eyes, so he picked up a napkin and gingerly offered it to her.

The gesture made her smile, and Jeanie softly spoke, "it's like we are on separate paths." She cleared her throat. "I thought that once the kids were off to school, we would have this wonderful life together while we were still young enough to do stuff. We were going to visit all the National Parks and go to Europe. We were going to visit every state in the union. We had so many plans."

"And, are you not doing that?" *That was a stupid question.*

"He went and bought this expensive boat. And not a little one either. I know he likes fishing, but come on!" Nick watched as a blue vein appeared on Jeanie's forehead. "He did it without even telling me. I came home from a meeting two months ago and there it was in my driveway."

Nick had no idea what to say. He sat there in silence, waiting. *Please keep talking. Please.*

"I'm not a fan of boats, in case you didn't notice. And we were supposed to use that money to travel."

Jeanie began to weep. "The worst part is that he never said a word to me before he bought it, because he knew I would give him push back." She was openly crying now. "That's the worst part. We used to talk about everything. It didn't matter what the topic was. We could talk about anything. We were never afraid of each other's feelings. We always worked through everything. For thirty-eight years. Everything."

"I'm sorry, Jeanie." Nick was surprisingly moved. He didn't know how to deal with his own compassion. He never realized he could feel that way. "Is there anything I can do?"

"You are doing it, just by listening." Jeanie tried to smile. "I'm afraid. I'm afraid that him doing this is a sign that our marriage is in trouble. I mean, not that he bought the boat, but that he didn't talk to me."

"It can't be that bad," Nick offered.

"I've been on the boat once. I tried. I got really sick and we were only out on the bay." Jeanie stopped to blow her nose in the napkin Nick had given her. "Excuse me, that was rude."

"Nah, come on." Nick reached for another napkin and handed to Jeanie.

"And we really don't talk much about anything anymore. If we do, we end up fighting." Jeanie wiped her eyes. "You know what? Enough of this. I need to get it together." She blew her nose one more time. "We'll work it out somehow. You don't just throw away a thirty-eight-year marriage."

No, I guess not, dammit. "No, you don't. Have you tried going to a marriage counselor?" Nick was conflicted. He wanted to tell her to leave him. He wanted to tell her he would show her the world, and do anything to keep her happy. But he also knew he didn't have the means to do any of that. He wanted her to be happy. That was the important part.

Jeanie looked down at her watch. "You know what Nick? I need to get going. It was really nice to see you. Maybe we can do this again, another time. In the meantime, I'll get going on this roommate idea and let you know what the committee works out." She stood at her chair.

Nick looked up at her. Mesmerized by her still, he sat motionless, flashes of past encounters with her teasing his brain.

"Nick? Did you hear me?"

"Oh yes, I'm sorry." Nick stood up. "My mind was wandering. Just remembering some things that I need to do this afternoon."

"Okay, so, I'll talk to you soon." Jeanie leaned in and gave Nick a kiss on the cheek and wrapped her arms around him in a gentle hug.

He didn't want to end the embrace, but the promise of another date heartened him to let go of her arms. "I'll wait to hear from you, then."

Chapter 19

Like watching grass grow, for God's sake. It's like watching paint dry. It's been three fucking weeks. She's not calling me. What the hell. This is for shit. I don't know why I expected anything different. She never gave a shit about me. And she was just being nice to me because I had a good idea to make her look good for that fucking event committee. Why do I always get my underwear tied in knots over her.

Nick kicked the side of the door as he walked to the back of his store. He had just thrown out some lady who wanted him to do some free prints with her paper directly from her phone. He was having none of it. He was in no mood. "Why do people think I'm here to do their shit for free? I have to make a living too. Nervy bitch." He kicked the door shut behind him.

Nick's mood had been dark for a long time. He had such high hopes of getting to spend some good amounts of time with Jeanie without her husband hanging around but he hadn't heard from her, not once, since their first coffee date. He had been encouraged by the fact that she wasn't too happy with her husband at the time. He felt a sliver of guilt for wanting the marriage to break up, but the feeling was fleeting, in pursuit of his ultimate goal.

The chair in the corner of his studio looked comfortable and inviting. He shuffled across to the chair and collapsed down into the deep cushion, throwing his head back. Nick stared at the ceiling for what seemed like hours, reminiscing, daydreaming and ultimately figuring out his next move.

His solitude was interrupted by his cell phone's angry ring. He had left it on the counter in the front of the store and wasn't in any shape to scramble out of the chair to fetch it, so he let it ring and eventually go to voice mail. "Ain't nobody that important that would call me that's worth the struggle of climbing out of this chair." He spoke out loud as if explaining away his malaise to someone in the room. "I'll get the voice mail later."

Nick put his head back down on the cushion, this time closing his eyes, and returned to plotting out what he wanted to do to further his mission. The phone rang again. This time, he forced himself up out of the chair to go answer it.

"What!" he shouted into the cell phone.

"Is that how you always answer the phone? Seems you need a little lesson in etiquette!" came a familiar voice.

"Jeanie? Oh, man, I'm sorry. I've been getting so many junk calls, and this morning the phone has been ringing incessantly. How are you?"

Nick was red in the face and perspiring profusely. He was caught completely off guard, having given up on Jeanie not five minutes ago.

"I wanted to tell you that the event committee thought your idea was great. We're even sending a second mailing... really just a postcard, about lowering costs by room-sharing." Jeanie explained. "I already signed you up with somebody, and put a $200.00 credit on your card. Do you remember Max Engel? He's coming alone."

"Can't remember him. That's okay, though. I only plan to sleep in the room." Nick paused. "That's great, Jeanie. Thank you."

"I thought that might be good news."

"It is."

"Um, Nick..." Jeanie paused.

"Yes?"

"I was wondering, if maybe... I thought maybe we could meet for coffee again. Or maybe lunch? Carl is going on an extended fishing trip this coming weekend."

"This weekend?" Nick didn't want to sound too eager.

"Yeah, if you have some free time."

"Let me look at my calendar. Can I call you back?"

"I guess so." Nick could almost hear the disappointment in her voice. "When will you know?"

"Hold on a second." Nick almost jumped over the counter to get to his appointment book. *Who am I kidding? Even if I have something, I'm going to cancel it anyway.* "How does Sunday for lunch sound?"

Jeanie's voice lifted an octave. "That would be terrific. Where can we meet?"

"Name the place and the time and I'll be there." Nick, once again, was making it as easy for her as possible. "I just have to be back in my studio by three."

"Well, then, let's go someplace near your office so we're not rushed. You like sushi?"

"Yeah, sure, and there's a cool place right on San Souci. Funny thing is its owned by Orthodox Jews, but it's the best sushi in the area."

"I know the place. Lady named Carol runs it." Jeanie chimed in. See you there at noon on Sunday.?

"Great, Jeanie. See you Sunday." Nick hung up the phone as his whole demeanor changed. He felt completely liberated.

* * * * *

Nick and Jeanie sat silently in the corner of the small Sushi Restaurant in Sans Souci Plaza on the quiet Sunday afternoon. There was only one other table being served and no background music. Neither of them felt comfortable talking. They sat, sipping tea and perusing the menu, doing everything they could to avoid eye contact.

"Okay, what'll ya have?" The boisterous owner stood too close to the table, her belly pressing up against the bottles of soy sauce and teriyaki. "How about a Bento Box. That'll give you a little bit of everything."

"That sounds good," Jeanie answered softly.

"One for me too," echoed Nick.

"Easy enough. You want Miso soup or a salad with that?"

"Miso for me," said Jeanie.

"Same here."

The waitress turned quickly. "I'll be back with some water and your soup in a sec."

Jeanie spoke up first. "I have to tell you, I'm a little uncomfortable doing this."

"Why? We're just having lunch. Two high school friends."

"I didn't want you to get the wrong impression. And I certainly don't want to run into anyone I know that might get the wrong impression."

"But there is no impression to get."

"Okay, as long as we're on the same page. I'm just so mad at Carl. Distraught, really. It's that damn boat." Jeanie took a sip of her tea, making a face. "Ick. Its cold already. Anyway, we had another huge fight over it. He tells me Wednesday night that he's leaving Thursday for a four-day excursion to the Bahamas on a fishing trip with a few of his buddies." She stopped for a second as someone came in the front door of the shop. After realizing it wasn't anyone she knew, she continued. "I mean, really. The night before he tells me. He's become so inconsiderate. He KNOWS how angry I am about the boat in the first place."

Nick was listening carefully. He wanted to be in a position to say exactly the right thing. He wanted to, for once in his life, be the voice of reason and sanity.

"I mean, am I wrong here? Shouldn't he have given me more notice, or even asked me if we had any other plans in place for the weekend? We didn't, but that's not the point. Am I right or wrong here?"

"Honestly, Jeanie, I think you're right. But you are driving yourself to distraction. You either have to accept the fact that he has and loves the boat or don't accept it. His passion for it will eventually wane, and I think the more you battle him, the more he'll use it as an escape." Nick was trying to be diplomatic. "If you accept it and use the time that he's away to do something that YOU really enjoy, you won't resent the boat or him as much."

"I guess that makes sense. But he hasn't once invited me to go with him except for that very first time." She interrupted herself. "Oooooooh. That's because I bitch at him about it all the time."

"Congratulations, Captain Obvious."

"Hey, that wasn't nice.'" Jeanie put her cup down, firmly in its saucer. "I did go out with him once, but I was still so angry at him for buying it without telling me that I barely spoke a word to him the whole time. And when we got home, he was just so happy to have been out on the boat with me, he was acting very amorous, and I, of course, was as cold as ice."

Nick sat quietly listening. *She's really unhappy. I'm not happy she's in such a bad place. I'm not. Yes, I am. If she ends up leaving him, I may have a chance. Dammit. That's not the way it should be. She should want to be with me.* He sat with his elbows on the table, his hands supporting his head, his eyes gazing into hers.

"And then just last week, I had to cancel plans we had for a few weeks because he was taking the boat up to St. Augustine, There was some kind of Legal Conference he never told me about. Normally, he would dread going to these things. He would fly in and out the same day. Last weekend it was a three-day affair." Jeanie motioned for the waitress by holding up her cup. "Any idea when our order will be ready." She looked over at Nick. "We've been waiting for quite a while, right Nick?"

Nick was caught off guard. He had been lost in thought, dreaming of what it would be like to have Jeanie. He had Carl out of the picture whatever way necessary, and was already moved in to her home, playing house.

"Huh? What?"

"Never mind. Do you need some more tea?"

"No thanks, I'm good." Nick thought further. "Can I get some water though?"

"Sure. And your Bento's will be right out."

Nick wanted to go right back to where they were. In his head, he was very happy. "Where were you?"

"Never mind. I probably shouldn't be airing my dirty laundry to you anyway." Jeanie retreated into her own head, and the two of them sat in silence, waiting for their lunch.

* * * * *

When Nick stopped to think about the conversation over lunch, he found himself tossing and turning in bed. Staring at the ceiling, he attempted to take himself back to the daydream that made him feel so good inside. He would wake up on a Sunday morning in a huge king-sized bed, roll over and see Jeanie asleep with the soft glow of morning sunlight that had crept through the blinds lightly bathing her face.

He would gently and carefully climb out of bed and sneak downstairs to the kitchen. There, he would put up a pot of morning blend coffee and put some cheese

Danish in the toaster oven to warm it ever so slightly. While the coffee was brewing, he would pull a flower from the arrangement on the breakfast table and slip it into a bud vase, placing it on the bed tray next to the napkin. When the coffee was done, he would pour a cup in Jeanie's favorite mug, slip the Danish onto a plate and place them both on the tray. He would skip up the steps being careful not to spill the coffee, walk in the bedroom, and softly sing 'their song,' to gently wake her.

Something sinister would interrupt his thinking. It was always just before Jeanie would wake up in his dream. *How the fuck can I get rid of Carl? He's in my way. Is this boat going to be enough to break them up?*

Nick would get out of bed and start pacing the apartment. He would stop and look at the stack of pictures of Jeanie to temper himself. His thoughts would then return to Carl and he could feel his anger rising. "How could this fucker mistreat my Jeanie? Why does she stay with him? There has to be some way to get this man out of her life. He's making her so unhappy."

As he walked back and forth through his apartment, his voice got louder as his frustration grew. Nick wasn't even aware that he was talking out loud. The voice in his head was where he usually figured these things out, but this time, his anger was palpable, and it was taking over his judgement, his reasoning, and his decision-making ability.

It was late December now, in the midst of the holidays, and Nick doubted he would hear from Jeanie again, at least until January, if at all, before the reunion. The obsession with this, however, was not going to let him rest. He had survived the holiday rush in his studio, and was somehow able to fill all the orders of family portraits, Christmas cards, postcards and gift items. He was flush with cash and had even put some money into his retirement fund.

The morning light was coming through the blinds in Nick's living room. That meant it was late enough to get going. Now that Christmas was past, the mall traffic would be slightly less. He decided that this was the day he was going to find out where Jeanie and that bastard lived. *I still have to figure out a way to get there without going up the boulevard, because those stupid people are going to be out returning or exchanging all the gifts.*

Nick threw some clothes on, poured some lukewarm coffee in his travel cup and hit the door. He decided to take his scooter instead of the car. The backfire would make too much noise. *One of these days I'm going to have to breakdown and have a fuel injection system installed if I'm going to keep driving that thing.*

Riding up 16th Avenue was the best way to get up through North Miami. It went all the way up to North Miami Beach. Nick rode over to 18th Avenue and then took that all the way up past Ives Dairy Road right into Highland Lakes. He had the address written in ink on the palm of his hand. His scooter was quiet enough to ride through the upscale neighborhood without being too conspicuous. He found the house at the back of the development on the main street. *These are huge houses. Carl must be doing really well for himself. I don't see a boat in the drive way... No cars... Maybe nobody is home. That's good. I'll leave the bike two doors down by this electrical box.*

Nick swung his leg over the bike and leaned it up against the street lamp pole. He took one last sip of his cold coffee, and replaced the cup in the holder. He glanced around to see that there was nobody around. He casually strolled down the street past the first house. He noticed the front door across the house open slightly, and a woman poked out her head. Nick immediately looked at his feet, and attempted to see what she was doing through the corner of his eye. The woman bent over and picked up a newspaper, returned inside, and closed the door.

Phew. That could have been a bit of an issue. Nick continued forward, and reaching the south side of Jeanie's house, ducked between the bushes and walked to the back of the house. He tried to look through some of the side windows, but they were all very high. He hadn't noticed that the house was elevated. He opened the back gate of the pool area, and slowly walked in. He knew the kids were away, and figured Carl was gone with the boat. If he got caught by anyone, he figured it would be Jeanie. He could talk his way out of that.

The sliding glass doors had vertical blinds inside, and they were all closed. Nick was having no luck finding a way in or even a way to look in. He continued on across the rear part of the house to the north end, where he found a two-step ladder leaning against the wall. "Aha, this might do the trick." He picked up the ladder and carried it with him, turning the corner to check out the north end. "This must be kitchen side."

Placing the ladder firmly on the ground, Nick reached around into his back pocket and pulled out a small digital camera. He carefully climbed to the top, and while he couldn't quite see in the window, he could tell there was no curtain, so he assumed it was the window over the sink. He reached up with camera and began snapping pictures.

"Keep your hands up and don't move."

"Huh?"

"Metro-Dade Police. Drop the camera and keep your hands up. Now step down the ladder and put your hands on the wall and spread your legs."

"I wasn't doing anything wrong, Officer."

"Right." The officer patted him down. He then took one arm and then the other, cuffing him behind his back. "You have the right to remain silent. Anything you say can and will be used against you in a court of law. You have the right to an attorney..."

"Wait, wait..." pleaded Nick. "I'm a real estate agent. This family is listing their house with me and I already have a buyer, but they're away. I wanted to show the buyer some pictures, that's all"

"Tell it to your attorney."

The police officer yanked on Nick's arm and pulled him out to the front of the house and helped him into the car. Nick noticed the neighbor across the street standing in her doorway watching.

Chapter 20

"Hey Telsky, I need some help."

"Who is this?" Telsky was startled by the phone ringing.

"It's me, Nick."

"Oh, Nick, man. What's up?" Telsky sat up in bed in his dingy studio apartment. Without opening his eyes, he knew it was early. His body was craving more sleep, but he knew this call was important because Nick never calls him. Nick hadn't even stopped by the store in years, since Andy died.

"Ya got any cash on hand. I need you to come bail me out. It's 500 bucks. I can pay you right back. I just gotta get out of here." Nick was whispering loud and fast.

"You get caught with a hooker?"

"No, you shit. I'll tell you later. Just come get me."

"Where the hell are you?"

"Dade County jail." Nick glanced around him and then added, "Hurry!"

He slammed the phone down just as the guard grabbed him by the arm and yanked him away from the desk. "Let's go, buddy. You're done there."

Nick didn't struggle. He had already lied to the arresting officer. He had to figure out how to get out of this mess without too much visibility. He had to come up with some kind of scheme that Jeanie would believe and not be too freaked out. *The last thing I needed was for her to get angry at me. Not now, not when I've finally gotten to be part of her world... her life.*

The guard did nothing short of shove Nick into a cell and slam the door behind him. "You'll have to wait here until you make bail. You're lucky. You got an easy judge. Now just don't make any trouble back here." The hefty built guard turned on his heels and strutted down the grey hallway, back through the double doors to the front desk.

Nick slumped down on the cement bench in the holding cell. *I guess this guy is right. At least I don't have to go to jail over this. I just hope Telsky doesn't fall back to sleep and forget that I called him. I am so fucking stupid. This is the dumbest thing I've ever done. Except maybe that time in Atlanta, this was taking a big chance. Those assholes better give me my camera back.*

Nick leaned back and rested his head against the cement block wall, either not noticing or not caring about the filth, grease, and blood stains all over the wall. His eyelids were drooping. The morning had taken a lot out of him, both physically and emotionally. Having been pushed around by the police officers and then the jail guards, he was sufficiently bruised. What hurt more was his pride and his psyche. He slowly gave in to his exhaustion and fell off to sleep, his head sliding down almost to his shoulder.

Nick was in a deep sleep very quickly, and as such he was, once again, dreaming of Jeanie and the life he would have with her. His dreams were always the same. This time, he had climbed back into bed with her, shared a breakfast in bed and when it was done, he began to nuzzle her at her neck. His passion became very vocal.

"Hey, asshole, shut up." Nick awoke with a start when the guard kicked him in the shin. "Nobody wants to hear about your wet dreams." The guard grabbed Nick by the collar and pulled him to his feet. "Come on. You made bail."

Nick shook his head like he usually did when he felt like he didn't understand what was going on or he thought his mind may be playing tricks on him. But it took him only a second to remember that he had been arrested. "Okay, okay, you don't have to drag me out... I got it when you dragged me in... But I'm in a hurry to get out."

"Don't be a wise ass."

Nick knew when to shut up. He walked quietly behind the guard, in lock step, down the dingy hallway to the double doors. The guard keyed in a four-digit code and the door opened. Nick poked his head around from behind the guard and saw Telsky standing at the desk. His pulse jumped as he sensed an end to the mess he had created.

"Hey man, what the hell did you get yourself into?" Telsky shouted from across the room.

Nick didn't offer any explanation until he reached the desk and could speak in a more civilized tone, or at least a quieter one. "I'll tell you later. Let me do what I have to do to get out of here."

The guard motioned Nick to the back corner of the counter. "Sign this here," he said, pointing to the bottom of a form. "Standard stuff. And sign here." He slipped another paper on top of it, one that had a lot of writing on it. "And one more."

Nick paused. "What am I signing. Wait. I want to know what I'm signing."

"Standard stuff, I said." The guard was losing patience. He leaned over to the clerk sitting behind the counter. "Don't you just love these assholes who have to read and know everything. These criminals who all of a sudden want to follow the rules." He turned his attention back to Nick, slapping him across the back of his head. "Sign it."

Nick signed the form. "Can I at least have my belongings back?"

"Can I at least have my belongings back...wah wah wah," The guard whined, mocking Nick. "That's one of the forms you just signed, asshole." Again, he turned to the clerk. "Josie, go get me number 6259."

Nick watched as the clerk got up from her chair and went out from behind the counter on the opposite side and went into a room marked "Authorized Personnel Only," Within seconds, she emerged carrying a small metal box back to her seat. She turned a few dials on the front on the box and it popped open. She reached in and pulled out Nick's wallet, watch. keys, phone and his camera. Nick let out a sigh of relief.

"Okay. Get your ass out of here. And stay out of trouble." The guard turned his back on Nick and left him standing there.

"I can go?" Nick asked.

Josie just nodded and returned to her attention to the computer screen in front of her.

Telsky volunteered an answer. "Yes. you jerk. Let's jet." He walked over and grabbed Nick by the arm. "Let's get out of this hell hole."

"Hey, quit pulling me around like a fucking jail guard." Nick was shoving his belongings back in his pockets. "Give me a second to put on my watch."

"You got time to do that in the car. Come on."

"Hey can you take me to pick up my bike?" Nick remembered that his motorbike was left leaning on the light post over on Jeanie's Street. "Although, maybe that's not such a good idea after all. The lady across the street from where it is… she's the one that called the cops on me. I'm sure of it."

As they climbed into Telsky's car, Nick related the morning's activities. "I had seen her watching me. Truth is, I probably shouldn't have continued on when I saw her. I just couldn't help myself…" Nick's voiced trailed off as he lost himself in his imagination once again.

"What are you talking about … you couldn't help yourself about what? Telsky was clearly confused. He hadn't seen Nick in a few years, but even he noticed a change in his demeanor. "You off your meds? Or just off your rocker, man?" Telsky looked over at Nick, who was leaning his head against the passenger side of the window and was staring outside. "Hello? You still among the living?"

No response.

"Nick, man, you okay?"

"Of course, I'm fine. Why?" Nick was genuinely surprised at the question.

"Telsky slowed down to a stop at a red light and turned completely towards his friend. "I don't know if you're just coming down off of something or if you just zoned out for a while... but I been tryin to talk to you and you were kinda spaced out."

"I was just thinking. That's all. Trying to figure out how to get out of this pickle I got myself into. That's all. Quit bustin my chops."

Telsky turned back and put his foot on the gas. "Excuse me for livin. Fuck you." He sped off down the highway southbound toward North Miami, and spoke not another word.

That was fine with Nick. He had to figure out how to do something preemptive so that things wouldn't get out of hand. *Maybe if I just call Jeanie and tell her I was in the area and wanted to stop by to say hey, but nobody was home. That I thought it was weird on a Saturday morning that nobody was home... that since she said she was having some issues at home I got worried... Nah, asshole. She'll never buy that. I've barely begun to build a relationship as a friend with her, why would I be sneaking around the back of her house so worried about her well-being? Well, it might work. It might just be a good building block to show how much I care.*

"Okay, we're here. There's your bike so get out."

"Geez, that's kind of you." Nick wasn't good at sarcasm.

"Hey, I was trying to do you a favor. It was you that bit my head off first."

"You're right, I'm sorry. It was nice of you to bail me out and pick me up. I'll drop the cash off at the store on Monday." Nick climbed out of the car.

"You realize that's tomorrow, right?" Now Telsky was being sarcastic.

"I get it. I spent a night in the slammer." Nick furtively glanced around. "Shit. That lady is at her damn door again." He openly waved to her, and then watched her quickly disappear. "You better go before she calls the cops on me again. I'll see you tomorrow."

Telsky pulled away quickly while Nick fidgeted with the lock on his bike. He couldn't get it unlocked fast enough. He wrapped the chain around his shoulders, hopped on, gunned the motor and hit the road. The last thing he needed was to get caught near there again. He did sign some stupid paper about a restraining order. Nick looked back over his shoulder to see if there were any cars in the driveway as he rode away. He hadn't taken the time to do that when he first got there.

The ride home was uneventful. Nick tried to keep his mind on pleasant things, although the reminder of his night in jail was ever present as his regular meds had begun to wear off. His hands were beginning to shake and he was feeling trembly inside. Anticipating the stomach cramps and impending diarrhea, he sped up. He knew exactly which medicine withdrawal was causing it. It distressed him that he was dependent on several drugs in order to function normally.

As soon as Nick parked his scooter, he didn't wait for the elevator, but skipped up the stairs to his apartment, anxious for the past twenty-four hours to be over. He fumbled with his keys to get in the front door, dropped his bag just inside the door jamb and went right back to the bathroom. He rooted through his bag of pill bottles and pulled out the lorazepam. Grabbing the glass from its shelf, he quickly filled it with tap water and promptly took a double dose. Then he took out a pill pack of the rest his meds and took them as well.

Nick had no other plans for Sunday so he found himself collapsing on his bed, fully dressed in yesterday's clothes. It took no time, and Nick fell off to sleep.

CHAPTER 21

"Meet me at the Denny's on Miami Gardens and 15th." Nick wasn't asking. He was demanding.

"Whoa. What the fuck?"

"Telsky, I need to talk to you. Don't want to do it over the phone." Nick was high, but he knew he had to get some kind of plan in motion. Telsky was the only one he knew who might be able to help him.

"What? Did you already use up all that you bought last week?" Telsky sat up in bed and glanced over at the clock at his bedside. "Geez, Nick. It's six in the morning."

"I know, I know, but I couldn't sleep. I need to talk to you. Meet me in an hour at Denny's, okay? Be there" Nick hung up.

Nick was fully dressed and pacing back and forth. If it weren't for the fact that Jeanie and her husband dropped the charges last month, there would still be a restraining order, and he would never have known how bad things were for her.

I really would rather not know how unhappy she is. I almost wish I hadn't gone over there last night. He screams at her unmercifully. He's brutal. He puts her down. Must make her feel so small. He better not be laying a hand on her. I'll kill him. That may be just what I have to do to get her out of that situation. It's that fucking boat, still, I bet.

Nick couldn't contain himself. He decided not to wait at home anymore. He grabbed his keys and headed out the door. There was a misty rain and it was threatening to do more, so he decided to take the Cutlass. It was mornings like this that he wished his car was a little quieter when he started it up.

"Aw fuck em." Nick said out loud as he turned the ignition key. BOOM. Another explosive backfire as he revved the engine. "Oh well," he added as he backed out of his parking space. He tried to pull away quickly as his car sputtering echoed through the back driveway of his building, in an attempt to avoid the barrage of profanity he normally got from some of his neighbors.

Guess I got up early enough that people were too tired to pick a fight this morning. Maybe I ought to just sell this thing. Nick pondered the idea as he drove up 16th Avenue. Arriving at Denny's a full half hour early, he sat in his car for a few minutes understanding fully that if he went in too early, he would most certainly overdose on coffee, and that wouldn't bode well for his anticipated conversation with Telsky.

After dusting off the dashboard, Nick began rustling through the glove compartment. He came across a few dogeared photos and some ancient receipts. There was nothing of real consequence, but he did find the yellowed ticket to the 'Sadie Hawkins Day Dance' from high school – that night that changed the course of his life; it was the night he ruined any possibility of the life of which he had dreamed. He sighed heavily and slipped the tickets back into the bottom of the glove box.

Nick sat for one more minute, lost in his memories. Startled by a hard rapping on the window, he looked up to see Telsky pressing his face against the car window. His heart pounded in his chest. He reached down and pulled the lever to open the door. Telsky leaned against it, so he couldn't push it open.

"Move you fucking moron." Nick's temper rose to the surface quickly. He flung his shoulder against the door just as Telsky stepped away sending him collapsing to the pavement, directly into a puddle. "Thanks, asshole."

"Hey, you're the one that woke me out of a sound sleep before even the birds were awake." Telsky reached out his arm to help Nick to his feet. "I'm really sorry, man. I really didn't mean for you to fall out of the car. I was just horsing around with ya."

"Wasn't funny. I'm serious, man." Nick brushed himself off. "Come on, I'll buy you breakfast, I need to pick your brain about something." Nick started towards the door of Denny's while Telsky lagged behind. Nick stopped and looked back. "What's the hold up?"

"Nothin', just have an old girlfriend that waits tables in there and I don't want a chance meeting." He picked up his pace to catch up. "She's probably not working no morning shift anyway, knowing her."

The two men walked into the restaurant together. There's something familiar about the smell of a Denny's, yet neither one could quite identify it. It didn't matter which store you entered in any city around the country. The smell of pancakes or grease; hamburgers or coffee, it was always the same.

Telsky whispered to Nick under his breath. "Let's just get a table in the corner in the back room." He practically pushed Nick to the right.

"Fine with me. I don't need anyone hearing what I have to say anyway." *Nick picked up the pace and headed directly back to the corner of the back room of the restaurant. I guess they use this for private parties, though I'd hate to be invited to a party here.* He slid into the booth by the back window. There was nobody else in the room. "Telsky, are we even gonna get served back here?"

"Yeah, the place will start to get busy soon. I'm sure they have someone already working this room." As soon as he said it, a crotchety old waitress half-walked, half-hobbled over to the table with menus in one hand and a steaming pot of coffee in the other.

"You need menus or you know what you want? Want coffee?" She started to pour before they had a chance to order. "You know about the 2-4-6-8 special?"

"Whoa. Slow down." Telsky was relieved, at minimum, that the server was not his ex, but he was still groggy and as such, was a little slow on the uptake. "I need a menu, please."

The waitress dropped the menus on the table. "I'll be back with the special menu."

Nick leaned forward. "So Telsky, I need your help." He reached for the cream, poured some in his coffee, and continued. "There's this woman I know, I mean, I've known her for a long time. And she's trapped in this shitty marriage, see? But she's afraid to leave the guy. He's so mean to her. She's always in tears." He took a sip of his coffee.

"So, what do you want from me?"

"Wait. Let me get through all this." Nick was interrupted by the waitress, who quietly returned, and promptly dropped the 2-4-6-8 menus on the table.

"You need more time?"

"Yeah, give us a couple of minutes, would ya?" Nick was a little coarse in his response. He turned back to Telsky. *How the fuck do I say this*? "I don't even know if I need you to do anything. I just want to pick your brain. Let me tell you what I'm thinking.'

Nick sat back and looked at the menu for a minute, deciding on some eggs and pancakes. He folded the menu up and put it on the edge of the table. Telsky did the same, hopefully signaling the waitress that they were ready to order. She got the message, came by and took their orders.

"Now, here's the thing. I want to get this guy out of the picture because I don't want this lady to hurt any more. Besides, I think I'm in love with her." Nick took a deep breath. "When I was in jail, I met some really rough guys in there. Thing is, I wasn't there long enough to make any connections. Reason I wanted to talk to you, was, well... I thought maybe you might know someone who knows someone... ya know, who could... well, kind of take care of the problem for me."

"Geez, Nick." Telsky blurted out.

"Shhh!"

"You're talking hit man?" Telsky whispered.

"I guess I am, sort of."

"There ain't no sort of about it. You just told me you want to have a guy knocked off." The color had drained out of Telsky's face. Nick wasn't sure if it was because of the subject matter he had presented, or a result of his previous night's partying.

Telsky leaned forward over the table and motioned to Nick to do the same. "What makes you think I would be able to help you with this, you little fuck? My only time in jail was because of minor drug charges. I ain't no hardened criminal."

Nick could feel the ants under his skin again. He suddenly felt queasy. "Hey man, I didn't mean to imply that you were capable of something like this. I just thought…"

"You thought wrong."

Telsky started to stand up.

"Don't leave. I'm sorry." Nick implored. "Please stay and talk." Nick stood as well, placing his napkin on the table. "I just want to talk to you. I was hoping to get some ideas or maybe some connections to people I could talk with."

Telsky sat back down. "Well, okay. Besides, I never pass up a free meal." Telsky slid back further into the booth and sat back. He picked up his coffee cup and took a sip. "What kind of connections are you talking about?"

Nick took another deep breath. "I just thought that maybe you met some guys while you were in the slammer that might be able to put me in touch with a hit man.... Just the kind of guy you described. Somebody who doesn't give a shit, who would make the hit for a few thousand bucks."

The two sat silent. Telsky fiddled with the spoon in his coffee, tapping it lightly against the sides, eventually falling into a rhythm. Nick picked up his spoon, and began tapping a counter-rhythm on the side of his cup, and before long the two of them were singing and tapping, and pounding on the table. Since they were still alone in the dining room, they were disturbing only their waitress who arrived at the table with the tray containing their breakfast.

"Okay, okay, Simon and Garfunkel. Cut it out and eat." She slid the plates onto the table. "You need anything else"

"Just a glass of water," said Nick. The waitress turned on her heels.

Both the men picked up their forks in unison and began eating, again in silence. Without the spontaneous music, they both seemed uncomfortable in each other's presence. After the waitress delivered the water to the table, they remained alone in the room for several guarded minutes. Slowly, the room filled with other customers, making further discussion impractical, so they finished their breakfast, Nick called for the check, and they left.

Outside the restaurant, Telsky gave Nick some hope. "I'll think on this for a while. I might be able to give you some direction. In the meantime, don't do anything stupid, like getting caught peeping again. Hear me?"

"Okay, fine." Nick extended his hand, but Telsky turned to walk away. "I appreciate anything you can do to help me out, Telsky." No response. Nick turned and walked in the other direction to his car. He got in and slammed the door shut. *Since when is Telsky so fucking sensitive? I didn't say anything so accusatory.*

Why did he jump down my throat? He wasn't gonna be putting himself out on a limb.

Nick put the key in the ignition and turned the engine over. *Hmmm, no backfire. That's nice for a change.* He put the car in reverse and backed out of the parking space. On the way home, he ran through a few scenarios in his head. Every single one of them ended up with Jeanie in his arms on some deserted island, drinking Mai Tais or Mojitos. Carl had either been kidnapped and murdered, killed and made to look like a suicide, or killed and made to look like an accident. The longer he thought about it, the more sinister his thinking was becoming. It was even beginning to startle him how evil his thought process could be.

When he had reached his apartment, Nick decided to distract himself so that he could relax his whole body. He had noticed while driving, that his hands were gripping the steering wheel so tightly that his knuckles were white. When he had finally gotten home and let go of the wheel, his fingers were numb. *Now that's not normal.*

Nick went straight back to the bathroom and pulled down all of his prescription bottles, dosing out his daily medications into a small paper cup like they have in hospitals. He doubled up on his anti-anxiety medication. He was beginning to do this on a more regular basis. It had kind of crept up on him over the past few weeks. This only bothered him when the pharmacist told him he couldn't get a refill on the prescription as early as he had wanted. He had to go three days taking the drug as prescribed as opposed to doubling up. When he saw the doctor that same week, he just asked him to increase the dosage a little because he was having a lot of anxiety. Then he asked his psychiatrist to do the same. He loved it when one doctor didn't know what the other was doing. Nick used an old-time pharmacy that wasn't using computers for this medicine, and since it was so cheap, he paid cash without putting it through his insurance. Worked like a charm.

After downing the pills, Nick stretched out on his bed and impatiently waited for the effects to overtake him. The more he tensed up, the longer it took. He tried everything he knew to take his mind off of Telsky and of Jeanie. Tossing and turning for over an hour, he finally fell off to sleep.

When Nick takes his meds regularly, morning naps are non-existent. When he doesn't, his naps are deep, his dreams intense. He was being chased this time. He couldn't get far enough ahead to even look for a place to hide. He just kept on running. The road didn't look familiar, nor did the gun in his hand or the blood on his shoes. He had no recollection of shooting anyone. In fact, he had no recollection of anything that had happened in the past few hours. The last thing he remembered was Telsky handing him two pills with some numbers on them. The number on the pills was something like 714. He did remember that it was either his mom or his dad's birthday... July 14th or 16th. He knew he had seen the number on pills before, but it had been so long since he had taken anything other than his prescriptions. He kept running.

The sound of the footsteps behind him had faded, so Nick cautiously slowed his pace enough to look back over his shoulder. No longer was anyone chasing him. He looked for the first alley into which he could slide to catch his breath. Just a few more feet, he thought, and he could plan his next move. He could feel his heart pounding in his ears. He found a break in the buildings, slid in and leaned against the cool brick.

A few feet away, Nick noticed a dumpster. He ripped off his tee shirt, and then used it to wipe off the gun. *Where the fuck did I get this? What have I done? I gotta dump this thing.* He wrapped the weapon up in the shirt and with wobbly legs, he walked the few steps over to the rusted-out dumpster, and tossed the shirt in, gun secluded. He also decided to dump his blood-covered shoes.

He had no idea where he was, but he knew he couldn't go out the same way he had come in. He squeezed his way past the dumpster and came out the other side into an alley littered with sleeping bags and cardboard lean-tos filled with slumbering bodies. He tip-toed through and around, looking for a pair of shoes that would fit him. As he reached the end of the alley, he came upon an empty sleeping bag, but around it, a wealth of rewards. He grabbed a flannel shirt and a pair of beaten-up loafers that were only a half size too big.

With his new-found wardrobe, Nick casually strolled out of the alley on the sunny side, and began to look for an open business or a telephone. He realized he had his cell phone in his pocket, so he stopped and pulled out the phone, dialing Telsky's number.

"Hey, man, I need your help."

"Again, with the 6:00 am wakeup call? You in jail again?" Telsky was not pleased.

"No. What the hell did you get me into?" Nick was truly baffled.

"Hey, I only gave you a name and a number. After that, I'm out. You got problems, they're your problems." Telsky yawned through his final comment. "I'm going back to sleep."

"Wait, Telsky. I have no idea where I am and I have no car. I need you to come get me." It was too late. Nick was talking to dead air. He hung up the phone and looked around his surroundings. He didn't see a street sign. The store in front of which he stood was numbered 675, so he walked toward the corner to see what intersection. He didn't even know in which city he had landed.

When he got to the corner, he not only found the street sign but there was a little coffee shop open. Nick walked in, sat down and ordered a cup of coffee. He suddenly slapped his pants to be sure he had his wallet. Relieved to find it, he added a piece of cheese

Danish to his order. "I know this is going to sound like a silly question, but what city is this?"

"Boy, you must of hadda rough night! You're in Ft. Lauderdale By-the-Sea. Really, just Ft. Lauderdale Beach. Just a few blocks to the east is the water."

"Thanks. Buses go down A1A?"

"Yessir, about every fifteen minutes."

Nick fiddled with his coffee while it cooled and ate the cheese Danish, although it was stale. *What the hell did I do? This wasn't supposed to be how this was supposed to work. My hands were supposed to stay clean. All I was going to have to do was get a hold of the cash: Half up front, and the other half after.*

Just as he was finishing up his coffee, his phone rang.

"Hello?"

"Hey, it's me, Telsky."

"Huh?" Nick was having a hard time clearing his head.

"Did I wake you?" Telsky sounded almost happy about it.

"I think so. I was having this really intense dream.:"

"Good. I'm glad I woke you for a change." Telsky gave Nick a few seconds. "I was thinking about what we spoke about this morning. I think I have a name for you, but I don't want to talk about it over the phone. Come by the store tomorrow, after work."

"Wait. We haven't moved forward on any of what we talked about yet at all, right?"

"Geez, man, we only met four hours ago." Telsky was extremely confused.

"Just wanted to be sure. That dream was too real."

"I can't deal with this shit. See you tomorrow after work at the store." Telsky hung up the phone immediately.

Nick sat up in bed, still holding the open phone. In a cold sweat, he leaned over the side to see his old sneakers tucked under the night stand, no blood. He finally let out a breath of relief, realizing everything was okay, for now, and closed the phone. He fell back on the pillow and stared at the ceiling with literally nothing in his thoughts.

Chapter 22

"Are you Argeo?"

"Who's asking?"

"I'm Nick L. Telsky gave me your name." Nick could feel his voice shaking. He was desperately trying not to stammer. "He said you could connect me to someone. I need some work done."

"What kind of work would that be, Mr. Nick L." Argeo was coming across somewhat sarcastic, but Telsky warned him about this.

"I need a large trash item removed." Nick stayed exactly to the script Telsky had given him. "It's more than the city can handle, and I was told you have a man with the expertise to do the job." *I hope I'm doing this right. Last thing I need is to fuck up now.*

"He's a specialist, if you know what I mean."

"I'm not sure I follow." Nick wasn't familiar with that part. It wasn't in the notes Telsky had given him. "Specialist?"

"That means, Mr. Nick L., that he charges a hefty fee for his services. I just want to be sure you are aware of that fact before you enter into negotiations with him." Argeo paused, looking over Nick's shoulder. He continued without making eye contact. "It would be a shame to waste his time. Or mine."

Nick swallowed hard. "Um, I'm uh, aware that the job is expensive. I'm quite prepared to pay top dollar." *What was I supposed to offer here? Shit, he threw me off. Uhhhhh.*

"Okay, then. I am prepared to negotiate on his behalf. You will not meet him. Bring me $7,500 in cash and a photograph of the "client." Argeo began. He opened his desk drawer and pulled out a yellow pad. "Write down the name and address here. Once we have your deposit, we will take care of your trash item. Once that is done, we will let you know and will expect the balance due within five days." He finally looked directly at Nick.

"That sounds exactly like what was originally described to me. Mr. Argeo, I am prepared to give you the deposit right now. Only problem is I do not have a photograph of the client. Just tell your client that he is the only adult male living at that address. Will that be sufficient?"

"Well, I don't know, now." Argeo saw that Nick meant business, having handed over the cash. "Not sure we can work without a picture."

Nick fumbled for his wallet. "Wait, I have an idea." He ran his fingertips over the credit cards and photos stuffed into all of the slots of his nylon and Velcro bifold. In the side section, he had a cache of pictures of Jeanie. Nick pulled out three of the more recent pictures. "How about if you give your man these? They are pictures of the target's wife."

"Hey. Hey, that's it, you can leave now." Argeo stood up and motioned toward the door.

"What? Did I do something wrong?" Nick felt panic from head to toe. His mouth was suddenly so dry he could barely form the words he wanted to say. "What did I do?"

"We have no targets here. Just clients." Argeo sat back down. Nice doing business with you. Now go.

"You're not keeping my deposit over this, are you?"

I guess that wouldn't be fair, now, would it?" Argeo snickered. "But who said dealing with me would be fair? I'm sure it wasn't that fashion model pothead that sent you to me. Now get outta here."

"I'm not leaving without my deposit or your word that the contract is still intact."

"Ya know, I like a guy who stands up for himself." Argeo stood back up and reached out his left hand for the pictures, while extending his right hand for a handshake.

My father always told me a handshake is a man's word. It's as good as a signed contract. Do I believe this guy? I mean it's a shitload of my money. Nick took a deep breath and handed the pictures to Argeo. He was still a little hesitant about shaking his hand. Summoning up whatever resolve he had left, he strained to reach his right hand into Argeo's. "Thanks, man. I'll wait to hear from you.

"Whoa, whoa, cowboy. There are still some details to talk about. You have to tell me a bit more besides an address and a picture of the dude's wife." Argeo put the tablet of paper in front of him on the desk and sat back down. He pushed a button on his phone console. "Two cups of coffee, Daisy. Bring everything." He then opened a drawer of his desk and pulled out a file folder, wrote something on the tab and put it to the side.

"Okay, first of all, what is the time frame that you want this piece of trash removed?" Argeo was meticulous about sticking to the code words.

"It's been hanging around way too long, so the sooner, the better. The neighbors shouldn't be disturbed on the weekdays, since it seems it's a working-class neighborhood. I guess it would be better on a weekend, if you know what I mean."

"No need to qualify. I get it. Weekend removal. Now, how soon. Next week? Next month? When?" Argeo was all business.

"Oh, um. Let's see. The first week of next month would be good. I think. Yeah. The first week of next month."

"You sure about that?"

"Yeah, no wait. The week after that would my birthday week, yeah, the first week in March would be good. Let's keep that."

"Okay, so the week of March 4th." Argeo flipped the calendar back to January. "That's a little over three weeks. That'll work." He wrote something down on the pad. "Now, you're absolutely sure the trash will still be there then... the city will not be removing the trash beforehand and it will definitely be there that week, right?"

"Right, I think. No, I'm pretty sure." *How can I be absolutely sure? I'm not the guy's fucking guardian angel. I don't know every single thing on his calendar.* "I know he goes boating over some weekends, and works locally during the week. That's all I know."

Argeo sat back in his chair. "Obviously, you are not supremely involved with this family and it's trash removal needs. We'll figure it out. If my man has any further questions, I'll contact you."

"Okay. That works for me." Nick stood up. "So, do you need anything else from me?"

"Nothing else for now. I'll be in touch." Argeo didn't stand up. A handshake on the deal was the last time he would touch Nick. He would only ever speak to him by phone again. To Argeo, this was merely transactional. He was not holding anyone's hand. He would take his ten percent and be done with it.

Nick felt weird leaving the Hialeah strip mall. *How did it ever get this far? It should never have come to this. Jeanie should have been mine all along.* He dug down deep in his pocket to find his keys as he walked solemnly to his car. He had just committed a crime. He had just entered into a conspiracy to commit a murder. Were there enough layers of people and contacts to insulate him from getting into trouble? He didn't know, and he didn't know how he felt about all of it.

Sitting in his car in the parking lot for an hour, Nick had plenty of time to contemplate the imminent. He seemed less concerned about the ramifications of his actions than he was of the promise of his future life with Jeanie. He hadn't noticed any change in his thinking. By this point, he didn't think what he was doing was wrong. It was merely an expedient way to accomplish a goal. But was there a time when he respected the institution of marriage? Did he possess a respect for the sanctity of human life? Was there some synapse that wasn't firing in his brain? He just wanted his Jeanie and he felt like he had waited long enough.

Nick finally, after much projection and daydreaming, put his hand on the ignition and turned the key. Again, the car exploded with a backfire. He quickly glanced around the parking lot to see if anyone had reacted. A few people were looking over at him but most were going about their business. Nick was startled by a sudden rap on the window.

"Hey fella, you could use a little work on this beauty. A fuel injection system to start." Nick turned around to see Telsky pressing his face against the window of his car.

"Fuck you. You scared the shit out of me." Nick could feel his heart beating in his ears. He reached down and tried to open the door but Telsky was leaning against it. "Move, dammit."

"What a stick in the mud." Telsky backed away from the car, raising his hands over his head, as if being arrested. "Who peed in your Wheaties?"

Nick pushed his way out of the car and shouted in a whisper. "Look, you little weasel, I'm freaked out enough. I don't need you busting my chops." Nick paced back and forth next to the car like a nervous father in the waiting room of the maternity ward. "I have to wait two or three weeks before this whole fucking thing is over and already, I can hardly breathe."

"Oh, cool your jets. All you have to do is cozy up to her. Make her feel like she can depend on an old friend, and she'll naturally reach out to you. Don't be doing pole vaults over a fucking mouse turd." Telsky leaned up against the car and lit up a cigarette. He took a long drag, letting the smoke seep slowly out of his nose and his pursed lips. "Call her. Meet her for coffee."

"Okay, jerk. Under what circumstances would I call her and take her out for coffee? Isn't it a little strange that out of the blue I'm asking her out for coffee?"

"No, man." Telsky took another drag of his cigarette. "You could just tell her you had some more ideas for that stupid reunion. You've been an event photographer for how many years? Haven't you seen some unique ideas that you can suggest?"

Nick dropped his shoulders. "That's not bad." He stroked his chin in thought. "She liked my idea of offering roommates..." He thought for a minute or two more. "Oooh, I could offer to supply backgrounds and props for some fun pictures at the banquet, or at least ask if she had thought about that... Maybe I could print up old black and white cut outs of our team uniforms, or backdrops from classrooms from the school and...."

"Whoa, whoa, Ansel Adams." Telsky stamped out his cigarette. "Chill." He shuffled around to the front of the car. "I'll leave you to your imagination. I gotta get back to my shop. Just find some way to get her confidence. I'm out."

Telsky hopped on his bike and was gone before Nick had come out of his stream of consciousness. *I have so many amazing ideas. Maybe I could go into business with Jeanie after this is all over. We could open up an event planning company. She knows all about the event details and I can handle the business end, and some of the extras.*

Nick spun around to say something to Telsky, only first finding that he was gone. *Shit, I did it again.*

Getting back into his car, Nick tried to figure out what he was going to say to Jeanie when he called her. He wasn't even sure she would be interested in going for another cup of coffee with him. That was unless, of course, her nasty husband was out on that boat of his. As he pulled his car out onto the boulevard, his phone started to vibrate. He had forgotten to turn the ringer back on. He decided to ignore it and see who called when he got home.

Chapter 23

Nick reheated the morning coffee in the microwave, even though it tasted like the bottom of the pot that had been sitting for five hours. After he finished gagging, he took his phone out to see who had called. He could have kicked himself. It was Jeanie. He didn't know why, but he took another sip of the coffee before he dialed her back.

"Jeanie, I'm sorry I missed your call. I was on my way home and I don't like to try to reach for the phone while I'm driving. What's up?" *Did that sound casual enough?*

"Not a problem. I just was calling to say hi. We've gotten a lot of great feedback on the roommate thing." Nick noticed something different in Jeanie's voice. It was kind of high pitched. There was something disingenuous, he thought.

"Are you okay?"

"Yes, why do you ask?"

"I don't know, you just sound different."

"I guess I can't put anything past you. Yeah, no, Carl blew me off this morning to go out on his boat. I had wanted him to shop for patio furniture with me. When he told me to get whatever made me happy, I told him that what would make me happy was if he would stay home for a weekend every once in a while." Jeanie took a deep breath and sighed. "It's like he didn't hear a word I said. It turned into a big argument and he went anyway."

"I'm sorry. Anything I can do to make it better? Can I take you to brunch tomorrow?" Nick asked hopefully, relieved that Carl had made this task easy for him.

"That would be nice." Nick could hear her sob through the phone. "I would like that."

"I have a great idea. Let's go down to the Biltmore. They have an amazing Sunday Brunch and it is so beautiful down there." Nick was remembering that he had the two free passes for brunch so it would only cost him gas, parking and tips and he could knock her socks off.

"Oh Nick, isn't that a bit much? I was thinking more like a bagel place closer to home."

"You have something else on your schedule?" Nick was doing his best to sound nonchalant.

"No, not really. Let me give you my address."

"I have it. I mean, isn't it the one on the return from the reunion invitation?" Nick didn't want to sound too eager.

"Yes, that's it. What time should I be ready?"

"I'll make a reservation for 11:00, so how about if I pick you up at, say, 10:15?"

"That sounds perfect."

"Okay, then, See you in the morning. Have a nice evening. Jeanie. Try not to stay mad. It's not good for you."

"Yeah, right. Thanks, Nicky. Night."

Before he could answer, Nick heard the click and dial tone. *Nobody ever called me Nicky before. Maybe she has a thing for me too. I think I'm going to get some of my ideas on paper. Maybe I should print up samples. Wait I don't need an excuse. This whole thing was her idea. Oh man.*

Nick jumped up, lifted up the cold cup of coffee and dropped it in the sink. For the first time in a long time, he felt something other than anxiety. It was a light feeling, one of anticipation, but it didn't carry with it the knots in his stomach of the palpitations in his chest and throat. It was a ticklish feeling in his stomach. It felt good.

* * * * *

"Where the fuck is that other copy of the yearbook? I don't want to tear up another copy. Shit!!! Nick was marching around his printing lab pulling shelf after shelf apart. His intention was to show up in the morning with not only his ideas, but printed materials ready for Jeanie to see, but the longer he rifled through his office and lab, the more his frustrations broke through. "God dammit to hell anyway." *She's not going to move any closer to me unless I can wow her with SOMETHING. It's not like she liked me that much back in high school. I gotta find a way to get her to trust me. To like me... to want to be around me...*

"Ah! Here it is." Nick started rifling through the yearbook, looking for well-remembered teachers from their physiques or their dress. He searched for favorite hang outs, carefully tearing them out of the book. Slowly but surely, he had a selection of four people and three backgrounds. He carefully set them up with lighting and photographed each picture. One by one, he thoughtfully fed the oversized printer with poster quality paper, and then carefully glued each one to foam board. When the cut outs were dry and done, he sat back and admired his work.

"These are amazing, if I say so myself. It's like being right back at high school. I think everyone will recognize Coach Seever, the Principal, Mrs. Blank and Mr. Mariconi, especially with the eraser in his hand. This should be pretty funny." Nick leaned back in the arm chair and closed his eyes, His body felt like it was melting into the worn leather and soon he was asleep.

Something made Nick jump up suddenly. He looked around in confusion, temporarily having lost his bearings, and not remembering why he was even at the store. He began, as he often did, slapping himself on the side of his head. *What the hell. What the hell am I doing here. What day is it? Why did I come here?* Nick only first realized that since he wasn't at home, he likely didn't take his medication, so his reaction was overblown. He tried to calm down by some deep breathing. *I'm okay. I'll be okay. This will pass.* He was softly spinning around in circles when he spotted the stack of cutouts by the front door of the store.

"Why do I always do this?" Nick walked over and looked through the pile, remembering everything except for the time. His heart palpations returned to normal as did his breathing, that is, until he noticed the clock on the counter. "Oh shit! How long was I sleeping?" It was already morning. Nick started rushing around to shut down all of his equipment and clean up his mess. He loaded up the cut outs into his car, having to fold down the back seat and tie down the trunk so he wouldn't have to fold the cutouts. The backgrounds, he had decided at printing, would be better off on easels and unrolled. All set to go, he jumped in the car and started it up. The backfire seemed louder than usual, but in a business district on a Sunday morning, Nick figured it shouldn't bother anyone.

Chapter 24

Nick took one last look in the mirror. His hair was clean and combed, his teeth brushed. He even surprised himself at how calm he looked. *I probably shouldn't have taken the second Ativan, but I don't think Jeanie would like the hyper me.* He picked up his keys and headed toward the door of his apartment, but realized it was only 9:15. *If I leave now, I'll end up getting there by 9:30, only 45 minutes early.* Nick thought better of it, though, figuring he'll show her the cut-outs before they go to lunch and maybe she'll want to store them at her house.

Skipping down the steps rather than waiting for the elevator, Nick recalled that he parked his car in the small garage area provided for residents. He had wanted to protect his handiwork from theft or vandalism. He used his security key to enter the back door. The last time he did that an alarm went off. He panicked and passed out that time, but later found out it had only been someone's car alarm and had nothing to do with him. It took three sessions of therapy for him to get over that and it had been over a year since he had parked there. He was unflappable on this Sunday morning.

His car had been left untouched. Nick secured the lines holding his artwork in place. He hopped into the car and gently turned the key, without putting his foot on the gas. He couldn't get the engine to turn over. Turning the key back, he pumped the gas a few times, not knowing if that would even work. He was just trying to get that old car started without making too much noise. He had already been warned twice. The third noise offense would mean eviction. He tried one more time to turn over the engine. No luck.

Nick shifted the car into neutral and opened the car door. With one foot out on the asphalt, he attempted push off and roll the car out of its space while steering it so he wouldn't hit anything. *One of these days I'm going to have to do something about this stupid car.*

Nick had worked up a sweat, having pushed the car through the garage and out through the lot, to the exit gate. He finally got in the car, turned the key and started it up, noise or no noise. Turning off onto Biscayne Boulevard, Nick drove as though he hadn't a care in the world. He never stopped to notice his dirty hands, his tousled hair or the wide and spreading wet stains under his arms. Early on Sundays, the Boulevard is quiet and traffic free, and a good time to drive with the top down, so Nick pulled off into an empty parking lot, pushed the automatic button, and hopped out, waiting to batten down and snap in the canvas top of his convertible. It was only then that he realized what a mess he was. *At least I still have a few minutes to clean up.* Nick looked around for some place that was open. There was a MacDonald's only a block to the north.

A face and hand wash, a quick comb and five minutes in front of the air hand dryer and he was good to go. By the time he was back in the car and on the road, he had figured out that he would be just about right on time.

Nick zipped up the road with an abundance of luck with traffic lights, reaching Ives Dairy Road at underpass, where he came upon an extremely long freight train. He could feel the ants under his skin crawling up his legs as each car passed slowly by. He tried counting them to pass the time but that didn't serve him well. It only reminded him of how long it was taking. Nick was never very good at waiting. After having counted over thirty, twice, and knowing that the train had already started before he got there, he concluded that it had over 100 cars just as he saw the last one chug by. *Finally! Fuckin train.*

Before the gate was up, Nick had his foot planted on the gas pedal. He took off, his car rattling over the rail tracks, and raced down Ives Dairy Road. He had come in from the other side the last time he was up this way, so he had to go to the end just before I-95 and turn right. He swerved into the right lane. *Dammit. My first red light.* He glanced down at the analog clock on the dashboard, forgetting that it had stopped working years ago, and he had never bothered to get it fixed.

There was only one other car at the light and it was right in front of him. As soon as the light changed, Nick leaned on his horn. The driver was quick to shoot him a bird as he pulled out into the intersection and headed toward the I-95 ramp. Nick cut the wheel hard and turned right onto the Highland Lakes

Boulevard, only to have to stop at the guard gate. *I don't remember having to stop at a guard gate the last time I came up. Oh yeah, I just rode around it on the sidewalk.*

The little old man in the little house slowly stood up, and then picked up his clipboard. He shuffled out of his nest and sauntered to the back of Nick's car. Nick tried to watch him through the rearview mirror. *What the hell?* Just as he could feel the hair beginning to stand up on the back of his neck, the gate went up and the little old man waved to him. Nick shot up his hand with no particular gesture, and drove through. There was something new on the road that wasn't there the last time he had ridden up the street, he noticed. Someone had installed speed bumps. *Another fucking aggravation. Between the stop signs and all these fucking humps, why would anyone want to live around here, It's a goddamn pain in the ass.*

Nick coasted down Highland Lakes Boulevard at 20 miles per hour. He didn't slow for the humps, nor did he stop for the stop signs. When there was only a block to go, he began to feel the twinges of anticipation. His mouth and throat felt dry, He found himself pursing his lips and sucking on his tongue. His breathing was faster, his heart pounding. He found the house, and coasted into the driveway. Jeanie's car must've been in the garage as there were no cars in the driveway nor on the street.

Nick hopped out of the car and walked up to the porch. He took one last deep breath, and glancing at his watch, he rang the bell. *Being only 10 minutes early isn't too bad.*

Nick heard a few clicks and clunks and just like that, the door swung open. "You're early!" Jeanie stood there, behind the screen door, in a lemon yellow, floor-length bathrobe. "Come on in. I need a few minutes to get some clothes on." She pushed open the screen.

"Um, I have a few things I brought for the reunion I wanted you to see. Let me get them from the car while you are dressing. I'll show them to you, and then we can head down to the Biltmore."

"That sounds good." Jeanie disappeared up the stairs.

Nick felt his heart fluttering in his chest as he untied the nylon rope on his trunk lock. He felt like a kid again. In fact, he felt like he did the night he walked up the path to Jeanie's front door for the very first time. The hairs on his arms stood at attention, tingling. He flipped the rope up over the trunk and carefully slid his treasured products out of the car, gingerly leaning them up against the bumper. *I sure hope she likes this idea.*

Jeanie met Nick at the door wearing a lemon-yellow chiffon blouse and a pair of white jeans. Nick was stunned by her beauty. *After all these years, she is still the most beautiful woman I have ever known.* "You look fantastic!"

"Oh stop. Come on in." Jeanie motioned Nick back to the family room, helping him carry his wares. "What is all of this?"

"I just had a great idea to add a little fun to the banquet part of your reunion," Nick began. "I've done this kind of thing for all kinds of events." He picked up the cut out of the football coach and but his face at the neck. "Don't you think all of the football players and a bunch of the people would like pictures taken with this?" He didn't give her a chance to answer. He unrolled the locker background from the ground floor of the school. "Wasn't this the big hangout in front of the cafeteria?"

"Oh, wow! I remember that! We all used to congregate there waiting for second shift for lunch. All the teachers in third period would let everybody out a couple minutes early so we could get down there and get in line." Jeanie stepped closer to the picture and pointed out her finger, counting to herself. Nick took the opportunity to move closer. "There it is. There's my old locker!"

"Everyone will have the same reactions you're having, Jeanie." Nick casually put his arm around her. "It'll be a big hit at the event." He pointed at the picture, too. "If you look really carefully, back in the corner on the right, you'll be able to see old lady Selma, the lunch lady. I think everybody remembers her. Everybody got exactly the same amount of french fries, and not one more."

Jeanie tossed her head back in laughter, landing it gently on Nick's shoulder. This was a moment that Nick had been dreaming of for the past forty years, but he knew he couldn't do anything about it. "You are so right. Oh my God, I remember that like it was yesterday." Jeanie turned to Nick. "How can I ever thank you. These are just fabulous." She leaned toward him and kissed him on the cheek.

Nick pulled away, in shock. Trying to hide both his surprise and his joy, he stuttered through his response. "Aw, come on, Jeanie. I would have done anything to help out. It's been so good to see you again." *Did that sound desperate? Did I sound like I was falling all over her?* Nick stepped back and nonchalantly began to roll up the backdrop. "I'm just glad you like them. I think we better hit the road if we're going to make that brunch reservation." Nick could barely get the words out with that noose around his voice box.

"You're right. You're absolutely right. Let me grab my purse." Jeanie disappeared down the hall into the kitchen, giving Nick a moment to compose himself. "I'll meet you at the front door."

Nick picked up the roll and leaned it up against the wall, and then picked up the rest of the materials to do the same. Upon lifting the last cut-out, Nick inadvertently knocked a picture frame off the end table. Thankfully for Nick, it landed face down on the fluffy throw rug. He picked it up and stared at it. It was Jeanie and Carl and their two daughters, from a long time ago, because the girls were young. *Jeanie looked so happy then. But its clear she's not happy now and dammit I'm gonna fix that. Wait, I could use this picture of Carl.*

"Hey, what's taking you so long?"

"I'm coming." *Shit, no time to take the picture. Oh well. They'll just have to stick to the original plan, and use the picture of Jeanie I gave them. Just get the guy who is with her.*

Nick and Jeanie talked very little in the car on the way down to Coral Gables. Nick had tuned into a radio station that played music only from the 1970's. and they both found themselves singing along. Occasionally, a song would stream out through the speakers that neither of them recognized and there would be a modicum of small talk... some about the past, some about the reunion, some about current events.

Finally, Jeanie stopped singing and talking and stared out the window. They had reached the end of I-95 and were headed south on U.S. 1. Nick was squirming behind the wheel, looking for something, the right thing to say.

"Hey, Jeanie," he started. "It may be none of my business, but..." He stopped, trying to detect her reaction. Sensing none, he continued. "Are you okay? I mean, is the same stuff going on? Or is it getting better? Or worse?" *I better just shut up now.*

Jeanie sustained her silence, not moving a muscle.

"I got it. You don't want to talk about it." Nick stared ahead at the traffic in front of him. Season in South Florida made driving unbearable. Part of the reason he never went anywhere was his tendency to blow up into road rage. He knew he had to be on good behavior, but he now had two triggers working against him: Jeanie's discomfort and the jackass who was riding his bumper behind him. *Be a gentleman. Don't lose your shit. Calm down. Think of a smooth lake in the morning with only the sound of the morning birds, skipping rocks. Sipping coffee and sitting on the dock, feet dangling in the water. Breathe.*

"You're very perceptive, ya know?" Jeanie finally spoke. After another moment of painful stillness, Jeanie began to slowly unfold her agony. "Nothing has changed. In fact, it's gotten worse. A lot worse. Carl loves that boat more than me. He even said as much. We had a huge fight on Thursday, and he told me he was taking the boat out with some buddies for the weekend." Jeanie took a deep breath. "I complained that he hasn't spent a weekend with me in months and I'm now convinced he likes the boat more than me, and he said that he probably does, because the boat doesn't nag him about anything. It doesn't demand anything of him. It doesn't tell him what he can or can't eat or what to wear, or where to be or when to be there."

Jeanie began to sob. Her words began to sound like a carousel, up and down, round and round. She would draw in a deep breath and spew a long stream of words until the air ran out, and then cry some more. "He. Didn't. Even. Say. Goodbye. Before. He. Left. This. Time. He. Was. So. Angry. All. I. Did. Was. Ask. Him. To. Be home. In time. For dinner on. Sunday."

"That's what set him off? Nick tried to just let her talk, but his heart ached for her. There must be something so much deeper than the boat. "Can I ask you a question?"

"Sure." Jeanie continued to sob.

"Is he having trouble at work, or maybe a health issue?" Nick was no therapist but even he knew there was something underlying in his anger. "What I mean is, maybe this isn't about you. Maybe he has something on his mind and he's just taking it out on you."

"How am I supposed to know? He never talks to me." Jeanie was coming out of her sadness and into anger. "It's like I don't even exist in his life anymore.

"Hmmm." Nick's mind began churning. Maybe there's someone else. Maybe the fucker is having an affair. "Is he acting different in other ways?"

"I'm not sure what you mean? Jeanie had finally gotten control of her sobs. Her words were soft and vulnerable now, as if she had surrendered to the enemy. "Nick, do you think you know what's going on in his head?"

Nick tread carefully. He could see that Jeanie was broken. Their time in the car was nearly over. This conversation wasn't something they could have over brunch. "I just think you need to slow down and try to hear what he is saying when you fight. Unless there is something going on with him, maybe you need to move in his direction a little." He paused. *What the fuck am I doing. I don't want to give her hope. I want her to come closer to me, not him.*

"You mean, what he yelled at me about? How I nag him? All that stuff? Jeanie's ire began to rise. Her rage became palpable. "You men all stick together, don't you? You know what? Let me out of the car. I'll take an Uber home."

While he had no intention of letting her out of the car, Nick took his foot off the gas, looking for a driveway into which he could turn. His hope was to redirect the conversation back to Jeanie and her strife. "Aw, Jeanie, I know you're just so unhappy," Nick offered as he slid his car into a parking space in one of the endless strip malls along U.S. 1.

Her face in her hands, Jeanie was crying uncontrollably. Her golden-brown locks fell forward as she lurched forward, doubling over into her lap. She gasped for air in between sobs. "No nobody body gets it." She took a deep breath. "My friends, my kids. They think, they think I'm making too big a deal."

Nick handed her his handkerchief. She continued. "Everyone can be so judgmental when they don't know what goes on behind closed doors." She gasped again. "Even the neighbors, who are only jealous of the boat, always dropping hints about wanting to go out with him."

"Look, Jeanie." Nick was way out of his league. He had no idea what to say or do. "Let me take you down to brunch. Let me just take you away from all of it, and get your mind off of all of this mess, if even only for a while." Nick hesitated, but eventually got up the nerve to reach over and gently rest his hand on Jeanie's shoulder. "Maybe you just need to escape for a few hours."

"You're sweet, but that's not my style." Jeanie picked her head up and looked directly into Nick's eyes. "I have to face the fact that my marriage might just be over."

"You really think it's that serious?" Nick's heart skipped a beat. "Don't you still love Carl?"

"I don't know." Jeanie looked away, out the window.

"Don't you think maybe you feel that way because you're feeling hurt right now?" *What the fuck, you asshole. This is exactly what you wanted.* Nick stopped talking and waited for an answer.

"Maybe, I don't know."

The silence was piercing. The two sat there, both fidgeting and both sighing. Nick finally broke the stillness. "Let's just go eat. We can continue the discussion, or not, but we can't just sit here. That okay with you?"

"Sure. You know what? You're right. Let's go and eat, and talk."

Nick turned the key in the ignition, shifted the car in reverse, and rolled back out of the space and they were on their way.

Chapter 25

"Nice ride!" The valet slid into Nick's car and slammed the door shut. He was grinning from ear to ear as he slipped the gear shift into drive and floored it.

Nick rolled his eyes and smirked as he took Jeanie by the arm. "I get that reaction a lot. I just registered the car as a Classic, and I only really take it out when I'm going to have a passenger. I usually ride around town on a scooter." Nick laughed out loud. "The kid wouldn't think my other ride was so nice."

They entered the high double doors into the lobby of the Biltmore Hotel in Coral Gables and followed the signs leading back to the champagne brunch. Nick had not requested indoor or outdoor seating. He figured he would leave that decision up to Jeanie.

"It's not too hot or muggy. I think if there's a table in the shade, I'd like to sit outside please." She looked hopefully to the Maîtres'. "This is just beautiful. I've never been here, even though I've lived in south Florida my whole life."

Nick was suspicious of Jeanie's tone. She was talking in this high ditzy voice. It reminded him of the girls he used to hate in high school... the ones who used to tease him, call him names. He whispered to her, "What are you doing?"

"Wait. Watch."

"I think we can accommodate you miss. Follow me." The Maître 'D picked two menus and strutted off down the hall to a pair of French doors. The two followed. When they reached poolside, the Maître D moved toward the awning and found a small table by a planter. He quickly removed a reserved sign from the table, holding it behind his back, and then pulled a chair out for Jeanie. "Please, sit."

Jeanie slipped into her chair, hanging her purse strap on the back. She allowed herself to be pushed in a bit closer and then turned to thank the Maître D. Nick, on the other side of the table, had seated himself and had already placed his napkin on his lap. When they were finally alone, Jeanie whispered across the table. "A little flirt goes a long way. Did you see me lean against him? That never hurts." Jeanie picked up her napkin and dropped it on her lap. "And that's how you get a table like this, and close to the buffet, to boot."

"Jeanie, I never knew that about you, you vixen!"

They laughed together.

"Care for a mimosa?" A tiny, tan and dark-haired server had approached the table. "It's our signature Sunday morning cocktail."

"Yes, please. How about you, Jeanie?"

"Love one. And I have a question. Is everything that's on the menu available at the buffet but just cooked to order?" Jeanie asked.

"Sort of. The buffet has a lot more, but is also a lot more money. You can can't special order anything from the buffet except there is an omelet station." The server stepped away from the table turned his head and coughed into his shoulder. "Excuse me, having some allergy issues. Do you need a minute or are you ready to order?"

Jeanie spoke up immediately. "Buffet for me." She smacked the menu shut and handed it to the server.

"Same for me, but may I have a cup of coffee as well?"

"Got it. Help yourself any time. All of the seafood is in the shade inside, along with the salads and omelet station." He pointed toward a cabana. "The dairy, cereals, cakes and fruits are over there, and beverages and beyond are over at the bar." He turned on his heels. "I'll have hot coffee for you before you get back."

"You go ahead and I'll watch your purse." Nick hadn't been on a date in decades, but he did remember his manners. "I'm enjoying the scenery"

Jeanie slid back her chair. "Thanks, you're sweet." She turned toward the seafood buffet, dropping her napkin on her chair. "As beautiful as it is, and as much as I love it, it's still a bit early for me to eat seafood. Think I'll go get an omelet to start." And off she went.

Nick couldn't turn away as he watched her serpentine through the tables back to the main aisle. *I am still so into this chick. Geez. It's been 40 years already. I remember those days when just the thought of her would bring on a boner, and I wanted to fuck her brains out. Now. I'm just happy to sit across the table from her and look into her eyes. Shit! Who am I kidding? I still want her. Bad. She's still got those long, slender, sexy legs. And a woman with perky tits after sixty? Aww shit.*

Nick could feel that familiar tingling between his legs. The beginnings of an erection... uncommon these days, unless he had that photo in front of him. That photo he miraculously got when he was stalking Jeanie at college, the one that he had taken by holding the camera over his head at her open window had proven to be, over his entire career in photography, the most well-timed picture he had ever taken. It had stopped time for him, capturing a simple image of Jeanie in front of a mirror, naked from the waist up, with her arms over her head, fiddling with her hair. It was so innocent, it was sexy. It was the genesis of hundreds of erections and fantasies.

Nick suddenly noticed Jeanie returning to the table with a plate in one hand and a glass in the other. He realized he had to do something to get rid of the telltale signs of his sexual attraction to her. His thoughts immediately went to Miriam Mayer...she was the ugliest chick in high school, and every time he thought of her, the thought of sex became repulsive. *Still works!*

Nick patted his lap to be sure before he stood as Jeanie approached the table. He took the plate from her and gently laid it at her place. He then slid her chair out for her, and then helped her push in closer. "That looks absolutely delicious. Did you get that in the Tiki Hut?"

"Yes. Right over there." Jeanie pointed to the Tiki Hut on the left. "Thank you, Nick."

"For what?"

"For doing this. For getting me out of my head." Jeanie paused, and swallowed hard. "For bringing me here and taking my mind off things, if only for a little while,"

"No problem." Nick turned and walked away. *This is going perfectly. I'm not pushing it. I'm taking it nice and slow and she's feeling gratitude. That's the first step. By the end of the morning, I'll have her just where I want her.... She'll call on me when she needs me.*

Over breakfast after a few more trips to the buffet and a few more Mimosas, Jeanie and Nick both reminisced and caught each other up with friends they had kept over the years. They talked about major life changes, politics, sports and current events. They argued and commiserated, they laughed and cried. When they knew it was time to leave, they were both feeling a strange sense of melancholy. Neither wanted it to end, however the server had dropped the check and had been back twice. He was approaching the third time, so Nick pulled out his wallet.

"This has been so much fun for me, Jeanie. We should do it more often." Nick pulled out the coupon and his credit card. Glancing over the bill, he laid everything back on the tray. "When Carl goes out on another extended trip, if you need a little company, maybe we can try another brunch somewhere else."

"I think I'd like that. Now that most of my friends have gone north to their summer homes, there aren't too many people around. I'll definitely call you." Jeanie began to put herself together. She pulled her purse off the back of her chair, and reached in to get her compact and lipstick. "Carl hasn't invited me to join him on the boat in months, I guess, because he knows I'm so angry at him about it. We could have bought a summer home too." She applied her lipstick pointedly. Nick could almost feel the anger building.

"Don't think about that. Don't ruin today by thinking about your anger." Nick tread lightly. "Just stay with me, here, now."

"You know what? You're absolutely right." She snapped the compact closed and twisted the cap on her lipstick. "I'm having a delightful time in spite of him."

The server returned to the table with the charge tray, and waited impatiently while Nick reviewed it, added a tip and signed it.

"Thank you, sir. Have a lovely afternoon." He reached over to pull out the chair for Jeanie.

"Hey man, no need to push us out the door. We're leaving." Nick stood up and walked around to help his date out of her chair. As they walked out to the main aisle, they both realized the place was mobbed. Every table was full, every buffet was crowded, and when they reached the lobby, there was a sea of hungry patrons waiting for a table. "Aha, that's why he wanted to get rid of us."

When the valet eventually brought his car around, it was sputtering. "Nobody knows how to handle this engine. He handed the driver a five-dollar bill. Did it explode when you started it?"

"Yeah, man, scared the crap out of me. Why does it do that?"

"Ah, my young man. Born long after the invention of the fuel injection system." He smiled at Jeanie. "That, young fella, was what they used to call a backfire."

"Oh, I hearda that." He looked down at his tip. "Thank you, sir.

Once they were down the driveway, Nick turned hopefully to Jeanie. "Do you want to take a drive through the Gables or maybe go over to Fairchild Gardens? Its early."

"No, really, thank you, Nick, but I have a lot to do for the reunion this afternoon. Because of your wonderful idea, we have a lot more singles coming. I have to start matching up roommates and booking rooms." She really seemed appreciative. "But thank you. I've had a very nice time. Maybe we can do something like that next time."

"Oh, okay. Is there anything I can do to help?" Nick did not want the day to be over.

"This is really a one-person job. But believe me I will definitely put you to work when I find a job for you! In fact, do you mind if I add your name to the committee?"

Nick could almost see his chest puff right out of his shirt. He was really feeling good about himself and how things were going. He decided not to push it any further. He still had two weeks to work his angle.

The Cutlass was still sputtering as they reached US 1. "I think we're sputtering because I need to get some gas. Do you mind if I stop?"

"I'd rather you stop now than run out of gas on I-95!." Jeanie said playfully.

Nick pulled the car into the first gas station he found. "Wait here. You can listen to the radio. It doesn't run off of the car battery."

Jeanie leaned over and turned on the radio. It was set to a satellite station from the 70's. She was awestruck.

The first song that came on was "Summer Breeze" by Seals and Croft. She rolled down the window. "Hey Nick, they're playing our prom theme song."

Nick smiled. *She doesn't remember that I wasn't at the prom. I guess that's good. She doesn't remember that I didn't have a social life in high school. Especially after that Sadie Hawkins Day Dance. God, it's like it was yesterday for me. Still makes my heart hurt. I guess it's a good thing she doesn't remember.*

When he was finished pumping the gas, Nick placed the nozzle back in the cradle. He grabbed a blue paper towel and wiped his hands. He wanted to be sure he didn't smell of gas when he got back in the car.

"Okay, we're good to go." Nick gently put his foot on the gas as he turned the key. Since the car had been running for a while, he didn't expect it to backfire, but he didn't want to take a chance. He shifted into drive and coasted to the driveway. He accelerated onto US 1 successfully and they were on their way. I-95 was only a mile away. They drove in silence as the sun flickered through the trees off the hood of the car. It was a soothing silence. It was comfortable. For both of them.

Chapter 26

"Hey, hey, is this Argeo?" Nick was whisper yelling into his phone. He was alone in his apartment, but still, he felt as though he was in danger just by calling this guy. "Argeo, this is Nick L."

"Yo! Mr. Nick L. I thought I told you we had your job on the docket and that you didn't have to or you shouldn't call here." Argeo was just a middle man but liked to talk tough.

"I just thought..."

"You thought nothin. I told you things are right on schedule for your pick-up." Argeo looked at his calendar. He used the swimsuit edition calendar from Sports Illustrated. He appreciated the female body, and found himself lost, staring at Miss March.

"But I wanted to know if you wanted a photograph of the actual item. Remember, I only gave you a photograph of the owner of the item."

"Oh yeah. You're the one who said take care of the item that she has with her. Nah. Fuh-get about it. That'll be fine." Argeo was still staring at the Miss March. "No sense you taking any unnecessary chances where you might get hurt. The item for pickup is on the schedule and that's it. Now don't call here again. I'm just the scheduler and dispatch."

Argeo hung up the phone. Nick stood there, numb, with a dial tone ringing in his ear. He slowly lowered his arm and snapped his antiquated flip phone shut. *I'm really going through with this aren't I? Do I really need this drastic a measure? Shithead. You won her over at brunch. You could probably have her in short time without having the guy offed.*

Nick began pacing through his apartment. He had only left Jeanie two hours ago, but the calm optimism he felt when he was with her was gone. He could feel every hair on his body begin to tingle, his heart fluttering in his chest. Soon, he felt the moisture beginning to form just under his hairline and in the crooks of his arms. The knot in his stomach was tightening, like a boa constrictor squeezes its prey. Back in the bathroom, Nick whipped open the mirror of his medicine closet and began rifling through the bottles. *Where the hell is it?* Spinning around, his eyes darted around the tiny room. He had a fixation on cleanliness, so the counters were bare. Suddenly Nick remembered where his pills were. He hurried out of the bedroom. As he had back-tracked in his mind, it came to him that he had taken a half pill before leaving for the big date. *Musta left them in the kitchen.* He opened the bottle and popped a pill under his tongue. *Need this to work fast.*

Flopping down on the couch, Nick crossed his arms over his head and closed his eyes, his elbows pointed toward the ceiling. A weird position, to be sure, but he knew that it would help him calm down quicker. He wasn't sure if it had something to do with blood flow or it was all in his head, but it worked. He started doing his breathing exercises. *Telsky saw me do this once and teased the hell out me. Called it Lamaze breathing like if I was having a baby or something. I can never let him see me do this again. Or anyone else for that matter. I ain't having a frickin baby. SHUT THE HELL UP TELSKY, YOU ASSWIPE. My chest hurts. No, it doesn't. It's just a little indigestion. I didn't need all those onions in that frickin omelet. Ooh I think my stomach is calming down. Where the hell is that box of tissues I had out here? Oh, right here.*

Nick sat up and reached to the end table, and picked at the tissue box. He wiped his brow of the perspiration that always forms when he's having an anxiety attack. But the inner talk was still going. *God, I hate this. Why would I be so freaked? I had a really nice time with Jeanie. I didn't do anything weird or dorky when I was with her, did I? She wouldn't have been so gracious and so amenable to going with me again if I had. My brain isn't working right again. I didn't leave my keys in the car again, did I? Of course not, asshole, you have your apartment keys on the same keyring. Settle down. You know this will go away soon.*

Nick laid back down and put his arms back up. His mind was taking him to dark places, imagining terrible things. He wriggled around to change his focus, trying to control his thoughts. He rarely had success. That's the reason for all of the medications. He often wondered why he had so many issues with his thoughts and feelings. His dad had never given him any solace. He had always been so tough on him.

Real men just shake it off and go on... like my little league coach telling me to rub dirt on my elbow and keep going when I scraped it sliding into second. "Be a man," Dad used to say to me. Never worked for Rick and apparently, it didn't work for me either. Ricky's dead and I'm all fucked up.

After a while, having relived his entire life in his mind, Nick dozed off to sleep. His slumber was fitful and disturbed. Had there been a witness, Nick would have been roused from sleep for fear something was terribly wrong. Within an hour, Nick was up again, pacing the apartment. While his anxiety had subsided, his guilt and remorse about the plans he had in place were still troubling him. *I wonder if I can still call this thing off, I know I can't call Argeo now. He would jump through the phone and strangle me if I called him twice in one day.*

Nick rolled over to his feet and decided to take his mind off of things. He picked up his phone and called Telsky. It was late afternoon, and although Nick had no idea of the exact time, he did take note of the palm frond shadow on his living room curtain. The sun had to be far to the west for that to be there, making it somewhere near dinner time.

"Hey man, wanna go grab a bite to eat?"

"You buyin?"

"Geez, don't you ever consider going dutch or pickin up the check for someone else?" Nick was annoyed, but he wanted the company. "Yeah, I'm buyin."

"Okay, pick me up in an hour," Telsky said quickly, and then hung up.

Nick was caught, again, with a dial tone in his ear. *This time he got angry. Is it me? Doesn't anyone have any fucking manners anymore? Why the hell does everyone hang up on me? My mother taught me better than this. I'm gonna roast his ass for that.*

Nick turned on the television. Nothing but basketball and some college baseball on. He sat back on the couch with the remote in one hand and his phone in the other. He flipped the stations back and forth looking for something worth watching. He kept stopping and looking at the phone, wanting desperately to call Jeanie. "Nope. Not gonna do it. Gonna do this right." He put the phone in his pocket, leaned back on the couch and put his feet up on the coffee table. "For once, I'm going to be normal."

* * * * *

Nick waited for five minutes before he hit the horn on the car the second time. Telsky made him wait every time he picked him up. It was a Sunday evening and all the stores were already closed on the street. Telsky was still sleeping in the back of the auto part store that he had inherited. He never married, never bought a home. He has never even lived in an apartment. He has always lived in a small room. Went from his parents' house where he shared a room with his brother to the closet sized space in the back of the store. He just didn't care.

Nick leaned on the horn a second time, and then waited again, this time doing the drum solo from Wipeout with his fingers on the steering wheel. His fingers moved rapidly, but after a while they began to throb. Finally, the passenger door whipped open. "Keep your shorts on, man." Telsky collapsed into the car. "Not like you gave me much time to get my act together for this soiree."

"You're such a pisser." Nick put the car in gear. "What do you feel like eating? Keep in mind your budget is not unlimited, like no Morton's, Joe's or Smith and Wolensky." Nick had already been through this conversation with Telsky. He had expensive taste in dining. The guy was used to running with drug dealers who had money to burn.

"I don't care. A good burger is fine with me... or Italian. You're driving. You pick." Telsky was still fumbling around with his seatbelt. "Did you have these things put into the car after the fact or are they factory.? What year is this again?"

"It's a sixty-eight. They're factory. They had to be. That was the first year they had to be by law." Nick glanced over at Telsky. "Why, what's your problem?"

"Nothin. Just had a little trouble getting it on, that's all." Telsky took a deep breath, sighed and settled in for the ride. "So, how's the master plan coming, whatever it is."

"Everything's fine. I had brunch with my lady friend this morning. Looks like everything's going to work out fine without any funny business." Nick was grinning like a child in front of a birthday cake. "I'm finally going to be with the only woman I have ever felt anything for."

Whaddaya mean, without any funny business? You know you can't call off the dogs now, don't you.?" Telsky was very serious.

"I can't? You mean they're going to go through with the 'pick up' even if I don't want them to? I can't stop it and get my deposit back?"

Nick's last comment left Telsky fascinated. He was in disbelief. It was incomprehensible to find that the one friend he had left, the one guy he thought had a modicum of success, was so naïve. "Oh pal, you have no idea what you've gotten yourself into. These are bad people. These guys would kill their own sisters for money. Not only are you not gettin your money back, but I guarantee if you try to call them, they'd rather shut you up and finish the job than let you lead the cops to them. They'll forgo the balance of the money to save their skins."

The color drained from Nick's face as he listened to Telsky talk. His breathing started to slow and get deeper and deeper. His head started swimming, and rather than pass out, he swerved the steering wheel and pulled into a gas station.

"You need gas?"

"No, I need air." Nick quickly left the car, gasping for breath. He hurried behind the car where Telsky couldn't see him, and began projectile vomiting. *Get a hold of yourself man. What the fuck have you gotten yourself into. You're not a killer. This is horrible. What have I done?* More vomiting. *What do I say to Telsky? He knows just enough to be involved. I should have waited and let nature take its course. She likes me anyway.* More vomiting. *She would have ended up divorcing him and reaching out to me. I won her over this morning. It was just a matter of time.*

"Hey, man. You okay back there?" Telsky had poked his head out of the car window and overheard the unmistakable sounds of puking. "You sound like me, last night, after my solo pub crawl." He laughed. "Man, I barely made it home. Fact, that's what took me so long to get ready for dinner." He sat back for a minute. Sticking his head out again, he added, "On second thought, when are we going to dinner? I haven't eaten anything yet today."

"Be right there." Nick could barely get the words out. He pulled a handkerchief out of his pocket and wiped his brow and then his mouth. He tossed it in the gas station trash can, not wanting to carry the odor of his stomach acid with him.

"Okay, let's go." Nick climbed back into the car. "Mind if we go to someplace like the Bagel Bar. I could really use a nice bowl of soup."

"That's fine. I can get a great deli sandwich there, right?"

"Yup." Nick drove in silence. He had to accept the fact that he made a terrible decision that can't be changed. It was going to take a lot of positive affirmations and likely a lot of his medication to get him through the next two weeks.

Chapter 27

Nick was aroused by the sound of his cell phone vibrating on the glass top of his coffee table before it even rang. He had fallen asleep watching the opening round of March Madness, although his interest in college basketball was marginal. He reached over blindly and picked it up, squinting at the tiny panel that revealed the number calling. He sat up suddenly, realizing it was Jeanie.

"Hello?"

"Nick," Jeanie said breathlessly. "I'm so glad you picked up the phone." She stopped for a second.

"Jeanie, you there?"

"Yes, I'm... I'm here." Again, there was silence.

"Are you okay?"

"No, Nick. Can you... Are you... Nick, something horrible has happened to Carl." She began sobbing into the phone. She couldn't speak further.

"I'll be right there." Nick hung up the phone without saying goodbye. *Ooh, I did it too. I guess there are times when it can happen to me. I hung up on her.* Nick grabbed his keys and was out the door. He tripped down the back stairway to the covered garage.

This was it. All he could do was envision her standing there with Carl's lifeless body and the police all over the place. He didn't care if his car made too much noise. He had to get there to comfort his Jeanie.

He turned north on to US-1 praying for green lights all the way up. *I have to be careful I don't speed or run a light. I just have to get there. Just calm down Nick. This is it. Just calm down.*

He held the steering wheel with one hand and frantically began patting down his pockets to be sure he had his meds with him. When he felt the familiar small square in the back pocket of his jeans, he let out a deep sigh. The past two weeks had been a long, drawn out spectacle for him. He had been waffling from anxiety and fear to depression, from wild anticipation to morbid devastation. He didn't know what to think. *What if she doesn't want me after all of this? What if she decides to be alone or pick somebody else over me? What if her daughters don't like me?*

The one thought that hadn't crossed his mind was guilt. The time that had passed had been spent mostly dreaming of his future with Jeanie, and not how it was going to become a reality.

Nick's prayers for good luck with traffic were not working. It seemed like an eternity until he finally reached Ives Dairy Road. When he took the exit ramp under the overpass he had to jam on the brakes. "SHIT. A fucking train!" He screamed as loud as he had breath to. He looked at the woman in the car next to him. Apparently, she was just as angry as he. She mouthed the words, 'I know, right?'.

Nick quickly turned away. His eyes fixed on the car in front of him. When the train gate finally lifted and the light turned green, he didn't have to lean on his horn. The lady next to him took care of that. However, when he put his foot on the gas, he floored it, and once again, his car objected, backfiring. Under the overpass, the sound of it could have been a gunshot.

Nick switched lanes into the righthand lane as soon as possible. When he reached Highland Lakes Boulevard, he almost took the corner off, turning right. He got through the security gate faster than usual. Driving up Highland Lakes Boulevard, he began to feel his heart throbbing in his throat. *Oh no, not now.*

He pulled off on the swale, and wiggled to get to his pill box. He fumbled with it to open it, and pulled out one tiny half of an Ativan. Throwing it to the back of his throat, he swallowed it dry. *By the time I park and go in, it'll be working, I hope.*

Nick shifted back into gear and coasted back onto the street. He didn't have to put his foot on the gas before he came to the first stop sign. He rolled right through it and then slowly accelerated. It seemed as though now, after everything that had happened, he was in no rush to get where he was going. Coasting along at twenty miles per hour, he rolled up to the second stop sign.

Unexpectedly, his phone, which was pressed against his chest in his breast pocket, began to vibrate. It scared him. He clutched it, sliding it up and out of his pocket. It was Jeanie again.

"I'll be there in 2 minutes. I'm on Highland Lakes."

"Thank God." She hung up.

Nick pulled into the driveway. Carl's car wasn't there. Nobody's car was there. There were no police. *Hmm. Wonder what's going on?*

Nick hastened his pace to the front door and rang the bell. He waited for a minute before Jeanie slowly opened the door. She looked small. Her shoulders were curved in as she held herself with her arms, almost as if she let go, she would fall to pieces.

"Oh, sweet Jeanie. What's the matter? What happened to leave you like this?"

"It's Carl."

"What did he do now?"

"No, it's not that." She started to cry.

Nick gently pushed his way in and put his arms around her. He let her cry. When she sobbed, he held her tighter; When she gasped and got a hold of herself, he let go.

"Thank you so much for coming. I didn't know who else to call." She leaned up against the archway in the foyer. "I was here all alone when I got a call from the police saying something happened to Carl. They weren't able to give me any details until they did more investigation. Now I'm waiting to hear back from them."

"Oh, honey, I'm so sorry," Nick offered. "Do you think maybe you want to get out of here for a little while? We can just go down and get a cup of coffee while you wait." Nick had a great sense of relief now that this whole thing was over. *Now all I have to do is step in and be her knight in shining armor.*

"I don't know. Maybe I need to just stay here."

"Whatever you want to do. I'm here to help. I just thought a change of scenery. They have your cell number, right?" Nick was gently pushing her, although he was fine with staying there with her.

"You know, you're right. I've been pacing around here for two hours already. I could use a cup of coffee." Jeanie looked hopefully up at Nick. "I think you have a good idea. Let me get my purse."

Nick leaned against the opposite side of the arch. "Take your time. I'm here for you and I have nowhere else to go." *I love you and I wish I never had to leave. Maybe I won't have to. Who knows?*

Jeanie came out of the kitchen with her purse and her keys. "I almost forgot my phone. Wait one more minute. I want to run upstairs and turn the lights off up there. Carl is a nut about leaving lights on."

"No problem. Take your time."

You can leave the lights on, the water running... you can do whatever the hell you want, as long as you're doing it with me, honey. I only want you. I'll bring you flowers and chocolates, and breakfast in bed every morning...

"Okay, I'm ready. Thank you for doing this, Nick." Jeanie opened the front door and started out. Nick followed. She turned to lock the door. "We were just starting to..." Jeanie dropped the keys. "Oh shoot," she interrupted herself. "These are Carl's keys. Can you drive? My car is in the garage and my keys are in the house."

"No problem. I have my convertible tonight." Nick leaned over to pick up the keys and then handed them to Jeanie. "Shall we? It's a beautiful night, too."

They walked down the path to the car in the driveway. Nick walked in front of Jeanie and opened the passenger door. Jeanie sat down in the car. "Wow, Nick, you've kept this car in perfect condition since High School." She swung her legs in and he closed the door.

Nick walked around to the driver side, opened the door and climbed in. "You need to put on the seatbelt, and I think you will enjoy the night air if you roll down the window as well. We'll soon be into summer and be forced to use the air." He slipped the key into the ignition and put his seatbelt on and rolled his window down too.

"You ready to go?" Nick asked.

Jeanie gave a half smile and said, "I guess so."

Nick turned the key in the ignition. The car had been sitting long enough that he had to give it some gas.

Suddenly, Nick slumped over the steering wheel, his chest hitting the car horn. Jeanie began to scream.

His car had backfired, or so she thought.

Chapter 28

Detective Harris came back into the interrogation room, shaking his head. "Your man Jimmy Telsky just confessed to the shooting."

Jeanie sat up straight, staring in disbelief. She tried to talk, but no words would come out. "I, whah... who... whaa..."

The detective sat down, once again, directly across from Jeanie. "This Telsky guy claims that Nick had hired a hitman to kill your husband, Carl. He had a whole plan worked out, but the hitman somehow thought Nick was Carl. Telsky said something about a picture of you."

Jeanie stared at the detective in disbelief, hanging on every word.

"So, anyway. From what this Telsky guy said, he knows or knew Nick pretty well and knew Nick's car would backfire. He followed Nick and found the hitman in the bushes across the street. He told the hitman he would take care of it."

"But, but, but... I thought you said they were friends." Jeanie was shaking by now. "I remember Telsky from high school. He used to bully everyone. But why would he shoot Carl? I mean Nick? I thought you said they were friends."

"I said they knew each other pretty well. This Telsky guy has a record. Minor stuff, but a record just the same. He claims that he had blanks in his gun, and was gonna try to fool the hired hitman. He said Nick was having second thoughts about having Carl knocked off." Detective Harris was jotting a few things down on his pad as he spoke,

"Telsky claims that's why he fired the gun when Nick started up the car, so the sound would be loud enough." He paused. "The hitman apparently stepped away from Telsky, being a little suspicious, and took aim, himself. He didn't care which bullet hit the target, as long as he saw him slump over."

Detective Harris sat back in his chair. "Here's the thing, though. When you both were in the car and Nick started it up, the car did, indeed backfire at the exact moment that Telsky fired the gun... the wrong gun. The hitman stood down and never fired."

Sitting back in his chair, a strange sneer crossed the detective's face. "It wasn't just the car that backfired. As it turns out, the whole thing...both Telsky and Nick's plan... backfired."

* * * * *

At that exact moment, Jeanie's phone rang. She pushed the speaker button only to screen the call. "Hi, this is Jeanie. I can't take your call right now. If you are calling about the reunion, please leave your name and number and I'll call you back as soon as possible. If this is a personal call, let me know and I'll call you back when I get the message."

Carl cursed her long-winded message. "Shit, Jeanie, there's blood all over the driveway. Where the hell are you?"

ABOUT THE AUTHOR

J T Fisher writes for people who have a hard time talking about what's on their mind. Her fourth novel, Backfired, delves into something with which many can identify... the concept of unrequited love. Every book she writes introduces the reader into serious concepts, but in a lighter, fictional way. In this book, she reaches beyond her normal genre and delves into cozy mystery, from the male point of view.

Her writing began as an empty nester blog to fill time that was previously spent tending to her husband and two children. As she wrote and gained followers, she decided to try pure fiction. Her topics are always relatable, derived from personal experience, and dropped neatly into fiction.

With two grown children, she now resides in Central Florida with one four-legged child named Mitzi, and her husband. She enjoys reading, writing, live theater and playing with her grandchild, Amelia.

www.ingramcontent.com/pod-product-compliance
Lightning Source LLC
LaVergne TN
LVHW012033070526
838202LV00056B/5484